Aunt Jane's Nieces
in the Red Cross

Edith Van Dyne

Aunt Jane's Nieces

in the Red Cross

Aunt Jane's Nieces

in The Red Cross

By

Edith Van Dyne

Author of "Aunt Jane's Nieces Series,"
"Flying Girl Series," etc.

1915

AUNT JANE'S NIECES IN THE RED CROSS

FOREWORD

This is the story of how three brave American girls sacrificed the comforts and luxuries of home to go abroad and nurse the wounded soldiers of a foreign war.

I wish I might have depicted more gently the scenes in hospital and on battlefield, but it is well that my girl readers should realize something of the horrors of war, that they may unite with heart and soul in earnest appeal for universal, lasting Peace and the future abolition of all deadly strife.

Except to locate the scenes of my heroines' labors, no attempt has been made to describe technically or historically any phase of the great European war.

The character of Doctor Gys is not greatly exaggerated but had its counterpart in real life. As for the little Belgian who had no room for scruples in his active brain, his story was related to me by an American war correspondent who vouched for its truth. The other persona in the story are known to those who have followed their adventures in other books of the "Aunt Jane's Nieces" series.

EDITH VAN DYNE

CONTENTS

CHAPTER I

THE ARRIVAL OF THE BOY

"What's the news, Uncle?" asked Miss Patricia Doyle, as she entered the cosy breakfast room of a suite of apartments in Willing Square. Even as she spoke she pecked a little kiss on the forehead of the chubby man addressed as "Uncle"—none other, if you please, than the famous and eccentric multi-millionaire known in Wall Street as John Merrick—and sat down to pour the coffee.

There was energy in her method of doing this simple duty, an indication of suppressed vitality that conveyed the idea that here was a girl accustomed to action. And she fitted well into the homely scene: short and somewhat "squatty" of form, red-haired, freckle-faced and pug-nosed. Wholesome rather than beautiful was Patsy Doyle, but if you caught a glimpse of her dancing blue eyes you straightway forgot her lesser charms.

Quite different was the girl who entered the room a few minutes later. Hers was a dark olive complexion, face of exquisite contour, great brown eyes with a wealth of hair to match them and the flush of a rose in her rounded cheeks. The poise of her girlish figure was gracious and dignified as the bearing of a queen.

"Morning, Cousin Beth," said Patsy cheerily.

"Good morning, my dear," and then, with a trace of anxiety in her tone: "What is the news, Uncle John?"

The little man had ignored Patsy's first question, but now he answered absently, his eyes still fixed upon the newspaper:

"Why, they're going to build another huge skyscraper on Broadway, at Eleventh, and I see the political pot is beginning to bubble all through the Bronx, although—"

"Stuff and nonsense, Uncle!" exclaimed Patsy. "Beth asked for news, not for gossip."

"The news of the war, Uncle John," added Beth, buttering her toast.

"Oh; the war, of course," he said, turning over the page of the morning paper. "It ought to be the Allies' day, for the Germans won yesterday. No—by cracky, Beth—the Germans triumph again; they've captured Maubeuge. What do you think of that?"

Patsy gave a little laugh.

"Not knowing where Maubeuge is," she remarked, "my only thought is that something is wrong with the London press bureau. Perhaps the cables got crossed—or short circuited or something. They don't usually allow the Germans to win two days in succession."

"Don't interrupt, please," said Beth, earnestly. "This is too important a matter to be treated lightly. Read us the article, Uncle. I was afraid Maubeuge would be taken."

Patsy accepted her cousin's rebuke with her accustomed good nature. Indeed, she listened as intently as Beth to the thrilling account of the destruction of Maubeuge, and her blue eyes became quite as serious as the brown ones of her cousin when the tale of dead and wounded was recounted.

"Isn't it dreadful!" cried Beth, clasping her hands together impulsively.

"Yes," nodded her uncle, "the horror of it destroys the interest we naturally feel in any manly struggle for supremacy."

"This great war is no manly struggle," observed Patsy with a toss of her head. "It is merely wholesale murder by a band of selfish diplomats."

"Tut-tut!" warned Mr. Merrick; "we Americans are supposed to be neutral, my dear. We must not criticize."

"That does not prevent our sympathizing with the innocent sufferers, however," said Beth quietly. "My heart goes out, Uncle, to those poor victims of the war's cruelty, the wounded and dying. I wish I could do something to help them!"

Uncle John moved uneasily in his chair. Then he laid down his paper and applied himself to his breakfast. But his usual merry expression had faded into one of thoughtfulness.

"The wounded haunt me by day and night," went on Beth. "There are thousands upon thousands of them, left to suffer terrible pain—perhaps to die—on the spot where they fell, and each one is dear to some poor woman who is ignorant of her loved one's fate and can do nothing but moan and pray at home."

"That's the hard part of it," said Patsy, her cousin. "I think the mothers and wives and sweethearts are as much to be pitied as the fallen soldiers. The men *know* what has happened, but the women don't. It isn't so bad when they're killed outright; the family gets a medal to indicate that their hero has died for his country. But the wounded are lost sight of and must suffer in silence, with no loving hands to soothe their agony."

"My dears!" pleaded Uncle John, plaintively, "why do you insist upon flavoring our breakfast with these horrors? I—I—there! take it away; I can't eat."

The conversation halted abruptly. The girls were likewise unnerved by the mental pictures evolved by their remarks and it was now too late to restore cheerfulness to the morning meal. They sat in pensive silence for a while and were glad when Mr. Merrick pushed back his chair and rose from the table.

As Beth and Patsy followed their uncle into the cosy library where he was accustomed to smoke his morning cigar, the little man remarked:

"Let's see; this is the seventh of September."

"Quite right, Uncle," said Patsy.

"Isn't this the day Maud Stanton is due to arrive?"

"No," replied Beth; "she will come to-morrow morning. It's a good four days' trip from California to New York, you know."

"I wonder why she is coming here at this time of year," said Patsy reflectively, "and I wonder if her Aunt Jane or her sister Flo are with her."

"She did not mention them in her telegram," answered Beth. "All she said was to expect her Wednesday morning. It seems quite mysterious, that telegram, for I had no idea Maud thought of coming East."

"Well, we will know all about it when she arrives," observed Uncle John. "I will be glad to see Maud again, for she is one of my especial favorites."

"She's a very dear girl!" exclaimed Patsy, with emphasis. "It will be simply glorious to—"

The doorbell rang sharply. There was a moment's questioning pause, for it was too early for visitors. The pattering feet of the little maid, Mary, approached the door and next moment a boyish voice demanded:

"Is Mr. Merrick at home, or the young ladies, or—"

"Why, it's Ajo!" shouted Patsy, springing to her feet and making a dive for the hallway.

"Jones?" said Mr. Merrick, looking incredulous.

"It must be," declared Beth, for now Patsy's voice was blended with that of the boy in a rapid interchange of question and answer. Then in she came, dragging him joyously by the arm.

"This is certainly a surprise!" said Mr. Merrick, shaking the tall, slender youth by the hand with evident pleasure.

"When did you get to town?" asked Beth, greeting the boy cordially. "And why didn't you let us know you were on the way from far-off Los Angeles?"

"Well," said Jones, seating himself facing them and softly rubbing his lean hands together to indicate his satisfaction at this warm reception, "it's a long, long story and I may as well tell it

4

methodically or you'll never appreciate the adventurous spirit that led me again to New York—the one place I heartily detest."

"Oh, Ajo!" protested Patsy. "Is this the way to retain the friendship of New Yorkers?"

"Isn't honesty appreciated here?" he wanted to know.

"Go ahead with your story," said Uncle John. "We left you some months ago at the harbor of Los Angeles, wondering what you were going to do with that big ship of yours that lay anchored in the Pacific. If I remember aright, you were considering whether you dared board it to return to that mysterious island home of yours at— at—"

"Sangoa," said Patsy.

"Thank you for giving me a starting-point," returned the boy, with a smile. "You may remember that when I landed in your country from Sangoa I was a miserable invalid. The voyage had ruined my stomach and wrecked my constitution. I crossed the continent to New York and consulted the best specialists—and they nearly put an end to me. I returned to the Pacific coast to die as near home as possible, and—and there I met you."

"And Patsy saved your life," added Beth.

"She did. First, however, Maud Stanton saved me from drowning. Then Patsy Doyle doctored me and made me well and strong. And now—"

"And now you look like a modern Hercules," asserted Patsy, gazing with some pride at the bronzed cheeks and clear eyes of the former invalid and ignoring his slight proportions. "Whatever have you been doing with yourself since then?"

"Taking a sea voyage," he affirmed.

"Really?"

"An absolute fact. For months I dared not board the *Arabella*, my sea yacht, for fear of a return of my old malady; but after you deserted me and came to this—this artificial, dreary, bewildering—"

"Never mind insulting my birthplace, sir!"

"Oh! were you born here, Patsy? Then I'll give the town credit. So, after you deserted me at Los Angeles—"

"You still had Mrs. Montrose and her nieces, Maud and Flo Stanton."

"I know, and I love them all. But they became so tremendously busy that I scarcely saw them, and finally I began to feel lonely. Those Stanton girls are chock full of business energy and they hadn't the time to devote to me that you people did. So I stood on the shore and looked at the *Arabella* until I mustered up courage to go aboard. Surviving that, I made Captain Carg steam slowly along the coast for a few miles. Nothing dreadful happened. So I made a day's voyage, and still ate my three squares a day. That was encouraging."

"I knew all the time it wasn't the voyage that wrecked your stomach," said Patsy confidently.

"What was it, then?"

"Ptomaine poisoning, or something like that."

"Well, anyhow, I found I could stand ocean travel again, so I determined on a voyage. The Panama Canal was just opened and I passed through it, came up the Atlantic coast, and—the *Arabella* is at this moment safely anchored in the North River!"

"And how do you feel?" inquired Uncle John.

"Glorious—magnificent! The trip has sealed my recovery for good."

"But why didn't you go home, to your Island of Sangoa?" asked Beth.

He looked at her reproachfully.

"*You* were not there, Beth; nor was Patsy, or Uncle John. On the other hand, there is no one in Sangoa who cares a rap whether I come home or not. I'm the last of the Joneses of Sangoa, and while it is still my island and the entire population is in my employ, the life there flows on just as smoothly without me as if I were present."

"But don't they need the ship—the *Arabella*?" questioned Beth.

"Not now. I sent a cargo of supplies by Captain Carg when he made his last voyage to the island, and there will not be enough pearls found in the fisheries for four or five months to come to warrant my shipping them to market. Even then, they would keep. So I'm a free lance at present and I had an idea that if I once managed to get the boat around here you folks might find a use for it."

"In what way?" inquired Patsy, with interest.

"We might all make a trip to Barbadoes, Bermuda and Cuba. Brazil is said to be an interesting country. I'd prefer Europe, were it not for the war."

"Oh, Ajo, isn't this war terrible?"

"No other word expresses it. Yet it all seems like a fairy tale to me, for I've never been in any other country than the United States since I made my first voyage here from Sangoa—the island where my eyes first opened to the world."

"It isn't a fairy tale," said Beth with a shudder. "It's more like a horrible nightmare."

"I can't bear to read about it any more," he returned, musingly. "In fact, I've only been able to catch rumors of the progress of the war in the various ports at which I've touched, and I came right here from my ship. But I've no sympathy with either side. The whole thing annoys me, somehow—the utter uselessness and folly of it all."

"Maubeuge has fallen," said Beth, and went on to give him the latest tidings. Finding that the war was the absorbing topic in this little household, the boy developed new interest in it and the morning passed quickly away.

Jones stayed to lunch and then Mr. Merrick's automobile took them all to the river to visit the beautiful yacht *Arabella*, which was already, they found, attracting a good deal of attention in the harbor, where beautiful yachts are no rarity.

The *Arabella* was intended by her builders for deep sea transit and as Patsy admiringly declared, "looked like a baby liner." While she was yacht-built in all her lines and fittings, she was far from being merely a pleasure craft, but had been designed by the elder Jones, the boy's father, to afford communication between the Island of Sangoa, in the lower South Seas, and the continent of America.

Sangoa is noted for its remarkable pearl fisheries, which were now owned and controlled entirely by this youth; but his father, an experienced man of affairs, had so thoroughly established the business of production and sale that little remained for his only son and heir to do, more than to invest the profits that steadily accrued and to care for the great fortune left him. Whether he was doing this wisely or not no one—not even his closest friends—could tell. But he was frank and friendly about everything else.

They went aboard the *Arabella* and were received by that grim and grizzled old salt, Captain Carg, with the same wooden indifference he always exhibited. But Patsy detected a slight twinkle in the shrewd gray eyes that made her feel they were welcome. Carg, a seaman of vast experience, was wholly devoted to his young master. Indeed, the girls suspected that young Jones was a veritable autocrat in his island, as well as aboard his ship. Everyone of the Sangoans seemed to accept his dictation, however imperative it might be, as a matter of course, and the gray old captain—who had seen much of the world—was not the least subservient to his young master.

On the other hand, Jones was a gentle and considerate autocrat, unconsciously imitating his lately deceased father in his kindly interest in the welfare of all his dependents. These had formerly been free-born Americans, for when the Island of Sangoa was purchased it had no inhabitants.

This fortunate—or perhaps unfortunate—youth had never been blessed with a given name, more than the simple initial "A." The failure of his mother and father to agree upon a baptismal name for their only child had resulted in a deadlock; and, as the family claimed a direct descent from the famous John Paul Jones, the proud father declared that to be "a Jones" was sufficient honor for any boy; hence he should be known merely as "A. Jones." The mother called her child by the usual endearing pet names until her death, after which the islanders dubbed the master's son—then toddling around in his first trousers—"Ajo," and the name had stuck to him ever since for want of a better one.

With the Bohemian indifference to household routine so characteristic of New Yorkers, the party decided to dine at a down-town restaurant before returning to Willing Square, and it was during this entertainment that young Jones first learned of the expected arrival of Maud Stanton on the following morning. But he was no wiser than the others as to what mission could have brought the girl to New York so suddenly that a telegram was required to announce her coming.

"You see, I left Los Angeles weeks ago," the boy explained, "and at that time Mrs. Montrose and her nieces were busy as bees and much too occupied to pay attention to a drone like me. There was no hint then of their coming East, but of course many things may have happened in the meantime."

The young fellow was so congenial a companion and the girls were so well aware of his loneliness, through lack of acquaintances, that they carried him home with them to spend the evening. When he finally left them, at a late hour, it was with the promise to be at the station next morning to meet Maud Stanton on her arrival.

CHAPTER II

THE ARRIVAL OF THE GIRL

A sweet-faced girl, very attractive but with a sad and anxious expression, descended from the Pullman and brightened as she found her friends standing with outstretched arms to greet her.

"Oh, Maud!" cried Patsy, usurping the first hug, "how glad I am to see you again!"

Beth looked in Maud Stanton's face and forbore to speak as she embraced her friend. Then Jones shook both hands of the new arrival and Uncle John kissed her with the same tenderness he showed his own nieces.

This reception seemed to cheer Maud Stanton immensely. She even smiled during the drive to Willing Square—a winning, gracious smile that would have caused her to be instantly recognized in almost any community of our vast country; for this beautiful young girl was a famous motion picture actress, possessing qualities that had endeared her to every patron of the better class photo-dramas.

At first she had been forced to adopt this occupation by the stern necessity of earning a livelihood, and under the careful guidance of her aunt—Mrs. Jane Montrose, a widow who had at one time been a favorite in New York social circles—Maud and her sister Florence had applied themselves so intelligently to their art that their compensation had become liberal enough to enable them to save a modest competence.

One cause of surprise at Maud's sudden journey east was the fact that her services were in eager demand by the managers of the best producing companies on the Pacific Coast, where nearly all the American pictures are now made. Another cause for surprise was that she came alone, leaving her Aunt Jane and her sister Flo— usually her inseparable companion—in Los Angeles.

But they did not question her until the cosy home at Willing Square was reached, luncheon served and Maud installed in the "Guest Room." Then the three girls had "a good, long talk" and presently came trooping into the library to enlighten Uncle John and Ajo.

"Oh, Uncle! What do you think?" cried Patsy. "Maud is going to the war!"

"The war!" echoed Mr. Merrick in a bewildered voice. "What on earth can—"

"She is going to be a nurse," explained Beth, a soft glow of enthusiasm mantling her pretty face. "Isn't it splendid, Uncle!"

"H-m," said Uncle John, regarding the girl with wonder. "It is certainly a—a—surprising venture."

"But—see here, Maud—it's mighty dangerous," protested young Jones. "It's a tremendous undertaking, and—what can one girl do in the midst of all those horrors?"

Maud seated herself quietly between them. Her face was grave and thoughtful.

"I have had to answer many such arguments before now, as you may suspect," she began in even tones, "but the fact that I am here, well on my journey, is proof that I have convinced my aunt, my sister and all my western friends that I am at least determined on my mission, whether it be wise or foolish. I do not think I shall incur danger by caring for the wounded; the Red Cross is highly respected everywhere, these days."

"The Red Cross?" quoth Uncle John.

"Yes; I shall wear the Red Cross," she continued. "You know that I am a trained nurse; it was part of my education before—before—"

"I had not known that until now," said Mr. Merrick, "but I am glad you have had that training. Beth began a course at the school here, but I took her away to Europe before she graduated. However, I wish more girls could be trained for nursing, as it is a more useful and admirable accomplishment than most of them now acquire."

"Fox-Trots and Bunny-Hugs, for instance," said Patricia with fine disdain.

"Patsy is a splendid nurse," declared Ajo, with a grateful look toward that chubby miss.

"But untrained," she answered laughingly. "It was just common sense that enabled me to cure your malady, Ajo. I couldn't bandage a cut or a bullet wound to save me."

"Fortunately," said Maud, "I have a diploma which will gain for me the endorsement of the American Red Cross Society. I am counting on that to enable me to get an appointment at the seat of war, where I can be of most use."

"Where will you go?" asked the boy. "To Germany, Austria, Russia, Belgium, or—"

"I shall go to France," she replied. "I speak French, but understand little of German, although once I studied the language."

"Are you fully resolved upon this course, Maud?" asked Mr. Merrick in a tone of regret.

"Fully decided, sir. I am going to Washington to-morrow, to get my credentials, and then I shall take the first steamer to Europe."

There was no use arguing with Maud Stanton when she assumed that tone. It was neither obstinate nor defiant, yet it conveyed a quiet resolve that was unanswerable.

For a time they sat in silence, musing on the many phases of this curious project; then Beth came to Mr. Merrick's side and asked pleadingly:

"May I go with her, Uncle?"

"Great Scott!" he exclaimed, with a nervous jump. "*You*, Beth?"

"Yes, Uncle. I so long to be of help to those poor fellows who are being so cruelly sacrificed; and I know I can soothe much suffering, if I have the opportunity."

He stared at her, not knowing what to reply. This quaint little man was so erratic himself, in his sudden resolves and eccentric actions, that he could scarcely quarrel with his niece for imitating an example he had frequently set. Still, he was shrewd enough to comprehend the reckless daring of the proposition.

"Two unprotected girls in the midst of war and carnage, surrounded by foreigners, inspired to noble sacrifice through ignorance and inexperience, and hardly old enough to travel alone from Hoboken to Brooklyn! Why, the thing's absurd," he said.

"Quite impractical," added Ajo, nodding wisely. "You're both too pretty, my dears, to undertake such an adventure. Why, the wounded men would all fall in love with their nurses and follow you back to America in a flock; and that might put a stop to the war for lack of men to fight it."

"Don't be silly, Ajo," said Patsy, severely. "I've decided to go with Maud and Beth, and you know very well that the sight of my freckled face would certainly chill any romance that might arise."

"That's nonsense, Patsy!"

"Then you consider me beautiful, Uncle John?"

"I mean it's nonsense about your going with Maud and Beth. I won't allow it."

"Oh, Uncle! You know I can twine you around my little finger, if I choose. So don't, for goodness' sake, start a rumpus by trying to set your will against mine."

"Then side with me, dear. I'm quite right, I assure you."

"You're always right, Nunkie, dear," she cried, giving him a resounding smack of a kiss on his chubby cheek as she sat on the arm of his chair, "but I'm going with the girls, just the same, and you may as well make up your mind to it."

Uncle John coughed. He left his chair and trotted up and down the room a moment. Then he carefully adjusted his spectacles, took a long look at Patsy's face, and heaved a deep sigh of resignation.

"Thank goodness, that's settled," said Patsy cheerfully.

Uncle John turned to the boy, saying dismally:

"I've done everything in my power for these girls, and now they defy me. They've declared a thousand times they love me, and yet they'd trot off to bandage a lot of unknown foreigners and leave me alone to worry my heart out."

"Why don't you go along?" asked Jones. "I'm going."

"You!"

"Of course. I've a suspicion our girls have the right instinct, sir—the tender, womanly instinct that makes us love them. At any rate, I'm going to stand by them. It strikes me as the noblest and grandest idea a girl ever conceived, and if anything could draw me closer to these three young ladies, who had me pretty well snared before, it is this very proposition."

"I don't see why," muttered Uncle John, wavering.

"I'll tell you why, sir. For themselves, they have all the good things of life at their command. They could bask in luxury to the end of their days, if they so desired. Yet their wonderful womanly sympathy goes out to the helpless and suffering—the victims of the cruellest war the world has ever known—and they promptly propose to sacrifice their ease and brave whatever dangers may befall, that they may relieve to some extent the pain and agony of those wounded and dying fellow creatures."

"Foreigners," said Uncle John weakly.

"Human beings," said the boy.

Patsy marched over to Ajo and gave him a sturdy whack upon the back that nearly knocked him over.

"The spirit of John Paul Jones still goes marching on!" she cried. "My boy, you're the right stuff, and I'm glad I doctored you."

He smiled, looking from one to another of the three girls questioningly.

"Then I'm to go along?" he asked.

"We shall be grateful," answered Maud, after a moment's hesitation. "This is all very sudden to me, for I had planned to go alone."

"That wouldn't do at all," asserted Uncle John briskly. "I'm astonished and—and grieved—that my nieces should want to go with you, but perhaps the trip will prove interesting. Tell me what steamer you want to catch, Maud, and I'll reserve rooms for our entire party."

"No," said Jones, "don't do it, sir."

"Why not?"

"There's the *Arabella*. Let's use her."

"To cross the ocean?"

"She has done that before. It will assist our enterprise, I'm sure, to have our own boat. These are troublous times on the high seas."

Patsy clapped her hands gleefully.

"That's it; a hospital ship!" she exclaimed.

They regarded her with various expressions: startled, doubtful, admiring, approving. Presently, with added thought on the matter, the approval became unanimous.

"It's an amazing suggestion," said Maud, her eyes sparkling.

"Think how greatly it will extend our usefulness," said Beth.

Uncle John was again trotting up and down the room, this time in a state of barely repressed excitement.

"The very thing!" he cried. "Clever, practical, and—eh—eh—tremendously interesting. Now, then, listen carefully—all of you! It's up to you, Jones, to accompany Maud on the night express to

15

Washington. Get the Red Cross Society to back our scheme and supply us with proper credentials. The *Arabella* must be rated as a hospital ship and our party endorsed as a distinct private branch of the Red Cross—what they call a 'unit.' I'll give you a letter to our senator and he will look after our passports and all necessary papers. I—I helped elect him, you know. And while you're gone it shall be my business to fit the ship with all the supplies we shall need to promote our mission of mercy."

"I'll share the expense," proposed the boy.

"No, you won't. You've done enough in furnishing the ship and crew. I'll attend to the rest."

"And Beth and I will be Uncle John's assistants," said Patsy. "We shall want heaps of lint and bandages, drugs and liniments and—"

"And, above all, a doctor," advised Ajo. "One of the mates on my yacht, Kelsey by name, is a half-way physician, having studied medicine in his youth and practiced it on the crew for the last dozen years; but what we really need on a hospital ship is a bang-up surgeon."

"This promises to become an expensive undertaking," remarked Maud, with a sigh. "Perhaps it will be better to let me go alone, as I originally expected to do. But, if we take along the hospital ship, do not be extravagant, Mr. Merrick, in equipping it. I feel that I have been the innocent cause of drawing you all into this venture and I do not want it to prove a hardship to my friends."

"All right, Maud," returned Uncle John, with a cheerful grin, "I'll try to economize, now that you've warned me."

Ajo smiled and Patsy Doyle laughed outright. They knew it would not inconvenience the little rich man, in the slightest degree, to fit out a dozen hospital ships.

CHAPTER III

THE DECISION OF DOCTOR GYS

Uncle John was up bright and early next morning, and directly after breakfast he called upon his old friend and physician, Dr. Barlow. After explaining the undertaking on which he had embarked, Mr. Merrick added:

"You see, we need a surgeon with us; a clever, keen chap who understands his business thoroughly, a sawbones with all the modern scientific discoveries saturating him to his finger-tips. Tell me where to get him."

Dr. Barlow, recovering somewhat from his astonishment, smiled deprecatingly.

"The sort of man you describe," said he, "would cost you a fortune, for you would oblige him to abandon a large and lucrative practice in order to accompany you. I doubt, indeed, if any price would tempt him to abandon his patients."

"Isn't there some young fellow with these requirements?"

"Mr. Merrick, you need a physician and surgeon combined. Wounds lead to fever and other serious ailments, which need skillful handling. You might secure a young man, fresh from his clinics, who would prove a good surgeon, but to master the science of medicine, experience and long practice are absolutely necessary."

"We've got a half-way medicine man on the ship now—a fellow who has doctored the crew for years and kept 'em pretty healthy. So I guess a surgeon will about fill our bill."

"H-m, I know these ship's doctors, Mr. Merrick, and I wouldn't care to have you and your nieces trust your lives to one, in case you become ill. Believe me, a good physician is as necessary to you as a good surgeon. Do you know that disease will kill as many of those soldiers as bullets?"

"No."

"It is true; else the history of wars has taught us nothing. We haven't heard much of plagues and epidemics yet, in the carefully censored reports from London, but it won't be long before disease will devastate whole armies."

Uncle John frowned. The thing was growing complicated.

"Do you consider this a wild goose chase, Doctor?" he asked.

"Not with your fortune, your girls and your fine ship to back it. I think Miss Stanton's idea of venturing abroad unattended, to nurse the wounded, was Quixotic in the extreme. Some American women are doing it, I know, but I don't approve of it. On the other hand, your present plan is worthy of admiration and applause, for it is eminently practical if properly handled."

Dr. Barlow drummed upon the table with his fingers, musingly. Then he looked up.

"I wonder," said he, "if Gys would go. If you could win him over, he would fill the bill."

"Who is Gys?" inquired Uncle John.

"An eccentric; a character. But clever and competent. He has just returned from Yucatan, where he accompanied an expedition of exploration sent out by the Geographical Society—and, by the way, nearly lost his life in the venture. Before that, he made a trip to the frozen North with a rescue party. Between times, he works in the hospitals, or acts as consulting surgeon with men of greater fame than he has won; but Gys is a rolling stone, erratic and whimsical, and with all his talent can never settle down to a steady practice."

"Seems like the very man I want," said Uncle John, much interested. "Where can I find him?"

"I've no idea. But I'll call up Collins and inquire."

He took up the telephone receiver and got his number.

"Collins? Say, I'm anxious to find Gys. Have you any idea—Eh? Sitting with you now? How lucky. Ask him if he will come to my office at once; it's important."

Uncle John's face was beaming with satisfaction. The doctor waited, the receiver at his ear.

"What's that, Collins?... He won't come?... Why not?... Absurd!... I've a fine proposition for him.... Eh? He isn't interested in propositions? What in thunder *is* he interested in?... Pshaw! Hold the phone a minute."

Turning to Mr. Merrick, he said:

"Gys wants to go on a fishing trip. He plans to start to-night for the Maine woods. But I've an idea if you could get him face to face you might convince him."

"See if he'll stay where he is till I can get there."

The doctor turned to the telephone and asked the question. There was a long pause. Gys wanted to know who it was that proposed to visit him. John Merrick, the retired millionaire? All right; Gys would wait in Collins' office for twenty minutes.

Uncle John lost no time in rushing to his motor car, where he ordered the driver to hasten to the address Dr. Barlow had given him.

The offices of Dr. Collins were impressive. Mr. Merrick entered a luxurious reception room and gave his name to a businesslike young woman who advanced to meet him. He had called to see Dr. Gys.

The young woman smothered a smile that crept to her lips, and led Uncle John through an examination room and an operating room—both vacant just now—and so into a laboratory that was calculated to give a well person the shivers. Here was but one individual, a man in his shirt-sleeves who was smoking a corncob pipe and bending over a test tube.

Uncle John coughed to announce his presence, for the woman had slipped away as she closed the door. The man's back was turned partially toward his visitor. He did not alter his position as he said:

"Sit down. There's a chair in the southwest corner."

Uncle John found the chair. He waited patiently a few moments and then his choler began to rise.

"If you're in such a blamed hurry to go fishing, why don't you get rid of me now?" he asked.

The shoulders shook gently and there was a chuckling laugh. The man laid down his test tube and swung around on his stool.

For a moment Mr. Merrick recoiled. The face was seared with livid scars, the nose crushed to one side, the mouth crooked and set in a sneering grin. One eye was nearly closed and the other round and wide open. A more forbidding and ghastly countenance Mr. Merrick had never beheld and in his surprise he muttered a low exclamation.

"Exactly," said Gys, his voice quiet and pleasant. "I don't blame you and I'm not offended. Do you wonder I hesitate to meet strangers?"

"I—I was not—prepared," stammered Uncle John.

"That was Barlow's fault. He knows me and should have told you. And now I'll tell you why I consented to see you. No! never mind your own proposition, whatever it is. Listen to mine first. I want to go fishing, and I haven't the money. None of my brother physicians will lend me another sou, for I owe them all. You are John Merrick, to whom money is of little consequence. May I venture to ask you for an advance of a couple of hundred for a few weeks? When I return I'll take up your proposition, whatever it may be, and recompense you in services."

He refilled and relighted the corncob while Mr. Merrick stared at him in thoughtful silence. As a matter of fact, Uncle John was pleased with the fellow. A whimsical, irrational, unconventional appeal of this sort went straight to his heart, for the queer little man hated the commonplace most cordially.

20

"I'll give you the money on one condition," he said.

"I object to the condition," said Gys firmly. "Conditions are dangerous."

"My proposition," went on Uncle John, "won't wait for weeks. When you hear it, if you are not anxious to take it up, I don't want you. Indeed, I'm not sure I want you, anyhow."

"Ah; you're frightened by my features. Most people with propositions are. I'm an unlucky dog, sir. They say it's good luck to touch a hunchback; to touch me is the reverse. Way up North in a frozen sea a poor fellow went overboard. I didn't get him and he drowned; but I got caught between two cakes of floating ice that jammed my nose out of its former perfect contour. In Yucatan I tumbled into a hedge of poisoned cactus and had to operate on myself—quickly, too—to save my life. Wild with pain, I slashed my face to get the poisoned tips of thorn out of the flesh. Parts of my body are like my face, but fortunately I can cover them. It was bad surgery. On another I could have operated without leaving a scar, but I was frantic with pain. Don't stare at that big eye, sir; it's glass. I lost that optic in Pernambuco and couldn't find a glass substitute to fit my face. Indeed, this was the only one in town, made for a fat Spanish lady who turned it down because it was not exactly the right color."

"You certainly have been—eh—unfortunate," murmured Uncle John.

"See here," said Gys, taking a leather book from an inside pocket of the coat that hung on a peg beside him, and proceeding to open it. "Here is a photograph of me, taken before I embarked upon my adventures."

Uncle John put on his glasses and examined the photograph curiously. It was a fine face, clean-cut, manly and expressive. The eyes were especially frank and winning.

"How old were you then?" he asked.

"Twenty-four."

"And now?"

"Thirty-eight. A good deal happened in that fourteen years, as you may guess. And now," reaching for the photograph and putting it carefully back in the book, "state your proposition and I'll listen to it, because you have listened so patiently to me."

Mr. Merrick in simple words explained the plan to take a hospital ship to Europe, relating the incidents that led up to the enterprise and urging the need of prompt action. His voice dwelt tenderly on his girls and the loyal support of young Jones.

Dr. Gys smoked and listened silently. Then he picked up the telephone and called a number.

"Tell Hawkins I've abandoned that fishing trip," he said. "I've got another job." Then he faced Mr. Merrick. His smile was not pretty, but it was a smile.

"That's my answer, sir."

"But we haven't talked salary yet."

"Bother the salary. I'm not mercenary."

"And I'm not sure—"

"Yes, you are. I'm going with you. Do you know why?"

"It's a novel project, very appealing from a humanitarian standpoint and—"

"I hadn't thought of that. I'm going because you're headed for the biggest war the world has ever known; because I foresee danger ahead, for all of us; but mainly because—"

"Well?"

"Because I'm a coward—a natural born coward—and I can have a lot of fun forcing myself to face the shell and shrapnel. That's the truth; I'm not a liar. And for a long time I've been wondering— wondering—" His voice died away in a murmur.

"Well, sir?"

Dr. Gys roused himself.

"Oh; do you want a full confession? For a long time, then, I've been wondering what's the easiest way for a man to die. No, I'm not morbid. I'm simply ruined, physically, for the practice of a profession I love, a profession I have fully mastered, and—I'll be happier when I can shake off this horrible envelope of disfigurement."

CHAPTER IV

THE HOSPITAL SHIP

The energy of Doctor Gys was marvelous. He knew exactly what supplies would be needed to fit the *Arabella* thoroughly for her important mission, and with unlimited funds at his command to foot the bills, he quickly converted the handsome yacht into a model hospital ship. Gys from the first developed a liking for Kelsey, the mate, whom he found a valuable assistant, and the two came to understand each other perfectly. Kelsey was a quiet man, more thoughtful than experienced in medical matters, but his common sense often guided him aright when his technical knowledge was at fault.

Captain Carg accepted the novel conditions thrust upon him, without a word of protest. He might secretly resent the uses to which his ship was being put, but his young master's commands were law and his duty was to obey. The same feeling prevailed among the other members of the crew, all of whom were Sangoans.

In three days Jones and Maud Stanton returned from Washington. They were jubilant over their success.

"We've secured everything we wanted," the boy told Uncle John, Beth and Patsy, with evident enthusiasm. "Not only have we the full sanction of the American Red Cross Society, but I have letters to the different branches in the war zone, asking for us every consideration. Not only that, but your senator proved himself a brick. What do you think? Here's a letter from our secretary of state—another from the French charge d'affaires—half a dozen from prominent ambassadors of other countries! We've a free field in all Europe, practically, that will enable us to work to the best advantage."

"It's wonderful!" cried Patsy.

"Mr. Merrick is so well known as a philanthropist that his name was a magic talisman for us," said Maud. "Moreover, our enterprise

24

commands the sympathy of everyone. We had numerous offers of financial assistance, too."

"I hope you didn't accept them," said Uncle John nervously.

"No," answered the boy, "I claimed this expedition to be our private and individual property. We can now do as we please, being under no obligations to any but ourselves."

"That's right," said Uncle John. "We don't want to be hampered by the necessity of advising with others."

"By the way, have you found a doctor?"

"Yes."

"A good one?" asked Maud quickly.

"Highly recommended, but homely as a rail fence," continued Patsy, as her uncle hesitated.

"That's nothing," said Ajo lightly.

"Nothing, eh? Well, wait till you see him," she replied. "You'll never look Doctor Gys in the face more than once, I assure you. After that, you'll be glad to keep your eyes on his vest buttons."

"I like him immensely, though," said Beth. "He is clever, honest and earnest. The poor man can't help his mutilations, which are the result of many unfortunate adventures."

"Sounds like just the man we wanted," declared Ajo, and afterward he had no reason to recall that assertion.

A week is a small time in which to equip a big ship, but money and energy can accomplish much and the news from the seat of war was so eventful that they felt every moment to be precious and so they worked with feverish haste. The tide of German success had turned and their great army, from Paris to Vitry, was now in full retreat, fighting every inch of the way and leaving thousands of dead and wounded in its wake.

"How long will it take us to reach Calais?" they asked Captain Carg eagerly.

"Eight or nine days," said he.

"We are not as fast as the big passenger steamers," explained young Jones, "but with good weather the *Arabella* may be depended upon to make the trip in good shape and fair time."

On the nineteenth of September, fully equipped and with her papers in order, the beautiful yacht left her anchorage and began her voyage. The weather proved exceptionally favorable. During the voyage the girls busied themselves preparing their modest uniforms and pumping Dr. Gys for all sorts of information, from scratches to amputations. He gave them much practical and therefore valuable advice to guide them in whatever emergencies might arise, and this was conveyed in the whimsical, half humorous manner that seemed characteristic of him. At first Gys had shrunk involuntarily from facing this bevy of young girls, but they had so frankly ignored his physical blemishes and exhibited so true a comradeship to all concerned in the expedition, that the doctor soon felt perfectly at ease in their society.

During the evenings he gave them practical demonstrations of the application of tourniquets, bandages and the like, while Uncle John and Ajo by turns posed as wounded soldiers. Gys was extraordinarily deft in all his manipulations and although Maud Stanton was a graduate nurse—with little experience, however—and Beth De Graf had studied the art for a year or more, it was Patsy Doyle who showed the most dexterity in assisting the doctor on these occasions.

"I don't know whether I'll faint at the sight of real blood," she said, "but I shall know pretty well what to do if I can keep my nerve."

The application of anaesthetics was another thing fully explained by Gys, but this could not be demonstrated. Patsy, however, was taught the use of the hypodermic needle, which Maud and Beth quite understood.

"We've a big stock of morphia, in its various forms," said the doctor, "and I expect it to prove of tremendous value in comforting our patients."

"I'm not sure I approve the use of that drug," remarked Uncle John.

"But think of the suffering we can allay by its use," exclaimed Maud. "If ever morphia is justifiable, it is in war, where it can save many a life by conquering unendurable pain. I believe the discovery of morphine was the greatest blessing that humanity has ever enjoyed. Don't you, Doctor Gys?"

The one good eye of Gys had a queer way of twinkling when he was amused. It twinkled as the girl asked this question.

"Morphine," he replied, "has destroyed more people than it has saved. You play with fire when you feed it to anyone, under any circumstances. Nevertheless, I believe in its value on an expedition of this sort, and that is why I loaded up on the stuff. Let me advise you never to tell a patient that we are administering morphine. The result is all that he is concerned with and it is better he should not know what has relieved him."

On a sunny day when the sea was calm they slung a scaffold over the bow and painted a big red cross on either side of the white ship. Everyone aboard wore the Red Cross emblem on an arm band, even the sailors being so decorated. Uncle John was very proud of the insignia and loved to watch his girls moving around the deck in their sober uniforms and white caps.

Jones endured the voyage splendidly and by this time had convinced himself that he was not again to be subject to the mal-de-mer of his first ocean trip. As they drew near to their destination an atmosphere of subdued excitement pervaded the *Arabella*, for even the sailors had caught the infection of the girls' eagerness and were anxious to get into action at the earliest moment.

It was now that Uncle John began to busy himself with his especial prize, a huge motor ambulance he had purchased in New York and which had been fully equipped for the requirements of war. Indeed, an enterprising manufacturer had prepared it with the expectation that some of the belligerent governments would purchase it, and Mr. Merrick considered himself fortunate in securing it. It would accommodate six seriously wounded, on swinging beds, and twelve others, slightly wounded, who might be able to sit upon cushioned seats. The motor was very powerful and the driver was protected from stray bullets by an armored hood.

In addition to this splendid machine, Mr. Merrick had secured a smaller ambulance that had not the advantage of the swinging beds but could be rushed more swiftly to any desired location. Both ambulances were decorated on all sides with the emblem of the Red Cross and would be invaluable in bringing the wounded to the *Arabella*. The ship carried a couple of small motor launches for connecting the shore with her anchorage.

They had purposely brought no chauffeurs with them, as Uncle John believed foreign drivers, who were thoroughly acquainted with the country, would prove more useful than the American variety, and from experience he knew that a French chauffeur is the king of his profession.

During the last days of the voyage Mr. Merrick busied himself in carefully inspecting every detail of his precious vehicles and explaining their operation to everyone on board. Even the girls would be able to run an ambulance on occasion, and the boy developed quite a mechanical talent in mastering the machines.

"I feel," said young Jones, "that I have had a rather insignificant part in preparing this expedition, for all I have furnished—aside from the boat itself—consists of two lots of luxuries that may or may not be needed."

"And what may they be?" asked Dr. Gys, who was standing in the group beside him.

"Thermos flasks and cigarettes."

"Cigarettes!" exclaimed Beth, in horror.

The doctor nodded approvingly.

"Capital!" said he. "Next to our anodynes and anaesthetics, nothing will prove so comforting to the wounded as cigarettes. They are supplied by nurses in all the hospitals in Europe. How many did you bring?"

"Ten cases of about twenty-five thousand each."

"A quarter of a million cigarettes!" gasped Beth.

"Too few," asserted the doctor in a tone of raillery, "but we'll make them go as far as possible. And the thermos cases are also valuable. Cool water to parched lips means a glimpse of heaven. Hot coffee will save many from exhaustion. You've done well, my boy."

CHAPTER V

NEARING THE FRAY

On September twenty-eighth they entered the English Channel and were promptly signalled by a British warship, so they were obliged to lay to while a party of officers came aboard. The *Arabella* was flying the American flag and the Red Cross flag, but the English officer courteously but firmly persisted in searching the ship. What he found seemed to interest him, as did the papers and credentials presented for his perusal.

"And which side have you come to assist?" he asked.

"No side at all, sir," replied Jones, as master of the *Arabella*. "The wounded, the sick and helpless, whatever uniform they chance to wear, will receive our best attention. But we are bound for Calais and intend to follow the French army."

The officer nodded gravely.

"Of course," said he, "you are aware that the channel is full of mines and that progress is dangerous unless you have our maps to guide you. I will furnish your pilot with a diagram, provided you agree to keep our secret and deliver the diagram to the English officer you will meet at Calais."

They agreed to this and after the formalities were concluded the officer prepared to depart.

"I must congratulate you," he remarked on leaving, "on having the best equipped hospital ship it has been my fortune to see. There are many in the service, as you know, but the boats are often mere tubs and the fittings of the simplest description. The wounded who come under your care will indeed be fortunate. It is wonderful to realize that you have come all the way from America, and at so great an expense, to help the victims of this sad war. For the Allies I thank you, and—good-bye!"

They remembered this kindly officer long afterward, for he proved more generous than many of the English they met.

Captain Carg now steamed ahead, watching his chart carefully to avoid the fields of mines, but within two hours he was again hailed, this time by an armored cruiser. The first officer having vised the ship's papers, they were spared the delay of another search and after a brief examination were allowed to proceed. They found the channel well patrolled by war craft and no sooner had they lost sight of one, than another quickly appeared.

At Cherbourg a French dreadnaught halted them and an officer came aboard to give them a new chart of the mine fields between there and Calais and full instructions how to proceed safely. This officer, who spoke excellent English, asked a thousand questions and seemed grateful for their charitable assistance to his countrymen.

"You have chosen a dangerous post," said he, "but the Red Cross is respected everywhere—even by the Germans. Have you heard the latest news? We have driven them back to the Aisne and are holding the enemy well in check. Antwerp is under siege, to be sure, but it can hold out indefinitely. The fighting will be all in Belgium soon, and then in Germany. Our watchword is 'On to Berlin!'"

"Perhaps we ought to proceed directly to Ostend," said Uncle John.

"The Germans still hold it, monsieur. In a few days, perhaps, when Belgium is free of the invaders, you will find work enough to occupy you at Ostend; but I advise you not to attempt to go there now."

In spite of the friendly attitude of this officer and of the authorities at Cherbourg, they were detained at this port for several days before finally receiving permission to proceed. The delay was galling but had to be endured until the infinite maze of red tape was at an end. They reached Calais in the early evening and just managed to secure an anchorage among the fleet of warships in the harbor.

Again they were obliged to show their papers and passports, now vised by representatives of both the English and French navies, but this formality being over they were given a cordial welcome.

Uncle John and Ajo decided to go ashore for the latest news and arrived in the city between nine and ten o'clock that same evening. They found Calais in a state of intense excitement. The streets were filled with British and French soldiery, with whom were mingled groups of citizens, all eagerly discussing the war and casting uneasy glances at the black sky overhead for signs of the dreaded German Zeppelins.

"How about Antwerp?" Jones asked an Englishman they found in the lobby of one of the overcrowded hotels.

The man turned to stare at him; he looked his questioner up and down with such insolence that the boy's fists involuntarily doubled; then he turned his back and walked away. A bystander laughed with amusement. He also was an Englishman, but wore the uniform of a subaltern.

"What can you expect, without a formal introduction?" he asked young Jones. "But I'll answer your question, sir; Antwerp is doomed."

"Oh; do you really think so?" inquired Uncle John uneasily.

"It's a certainty, although I hate to admit it. We at the rear are not very well posted on what is taking place over in Belgium, but it's said the bombardment of Antwerp began yesterday and it's impossible for the place to hold out for long. Perhaps even now the city has fallen under the terrific bombardment."

There was something thrilling in the suggestion.

"And then?" asked Jones, almost breathlessly.

The man gave a typical British shrug.

"Then we fellows will find work to do," he replied. "But it is better to fight than to eat our hearts out by watching and waiting. We're the reserves, you know, and we've hardly smelled powder yet."

After conversing with several of the soldiers and civilians—the latter being mostly too unnerved to talk coherently—the Americans made their way back to the quay with heavy hearts. They threaded lanes filled with sobbing women, many of whom had frightened children clinging to their skirts, passed groups of old men and boys who were visibly trembling with trepidation and stood aside for ranks of brisk soldiery who marched with an alertness that was in strong contrast with the terrified attitude of the citizens. There was war in the air—fierce, relentless war in every word and action they encountered—and it had the effect of depressing the newcomers.

That night an earnest conference was held aboard the *Arabella*.

"As I understand it, here is the gist of the situation," began Ajo. "The line of battle along the Aisne is stationary—for the present, at least. Both sides are firmly entrenched and it's going to be a long, hard fight. Antwerp is being bombarded, and although it's a powerful fortress, the general opinion is that it can't hold out for long. If it falls, there will be a rush of Germans down this coast, first to capture Dunkirk, a few miles above here, and then Calais itself."

"In other words," continued Uncle John, "this is likely to be the most important battleground for the next few weeks. Now, the question to decide is this: Shall we disembark our ambulances and run them across to Arras, beginning our work behind the French trenches, or go on to Dunkirk, where we are likely to plunge into the thickest of the war? We're not fighters, you know, but noncombatants, bent on an errand of mercy. There are wounded everywhere."

They considered this for a long time without reaching a decision, for there were some in the party to argue on either side of the question. Uncle John continued to favor the trenches, as the safest position for his girls to work; but the girls themselves, realizing little of the dangers to be encountered, preferred to follow the fortunes of the Belgians.

"They've been so brave and noble, these people of Belgium," said Beth, "that I would take more pleasure in helping them than any other branch of the allied armies."

"But, my dear, there's a mere handful of them left," protested her uncle. "I'm told that at Dunkirk there is still a remnant of the Belgian army—very badly equipped—but most of the remaining force is with King Albert in Antwerp. If the place falls they will either be made prisoners by the Germans or they may escape into Holland, where their fighting days will be ended for the rest of the war. However, there is no need to decide this important question to-night. To-morrow I am to see the French commandant and I will get his advice."

The interview with the French commandant of Calais, which was readily accorded the Americans, proved very unsatisfactory. The general had just received reports that Antwerp was in flames and the greater part of the city already demolished by the huge forty-two-centimetre guns of the Germans. The fate of King Albert's army was worrying him exceedingly and he was therefore in little mood for conversation.

The American consul could do little to assist them. After the matter was explained to him, he said:

"I advise you to wait a few days for your decision. Perhaps a day— an hour—will change the whole angle of the war. Strange portents are in the air; no one knows what will happen next. Come to me, from time to time, and I will give you all the information I secure."

Dr. Gys had accompanied Jones and Mr. Merrick into Calais to-day, and while he had little to say during the various interviews his observations were shrewd and comprehensive. When they returned to the deck of the *Arabella*, Gys said to the girls:

"There is nothing worth while for us to do here. The only wounded I saw were a few Frenchmen parading their bandaged heads and hands for the admiration of the women. The hospitals are well organized and quite full, it is true, but I'm told that no more wounded are being sent here. The Sisters of Mercy and the regular French Red Cross force seem very competent to handle the situation, and there are two government hospital ships already anchored in this port. We would only be butting in to offer our services. But down the line, from Arras south, there is real war in the trenches and many are falling every day. Arras is less than fifty miles from here— a two or three hours' run for our ambulances—and we could bring the wounded here and care for them as we originally intended."

"Fifty miles is a long distance for a wounded man to travel," objected Maud.

"True," said the doctor, "but the roads are excellent."

"Remember those swinging cots," said Ajo.

"We might try it," said Patsy, anxious to be doing something. "Couldn't we start to-morrow for Arras, Uncle?"

"It occurs to me that we must first find a chauffeur," answered Mr. Merrick, "and from my impressions of the inhabitants of Calais, that will prove a difficult task."

"Why?"

"Every man jack of 'em is scared stiff," said Ajo, with a laugh. "But we might ask the commandant to recommend someone. The old boy seems friendly enough."

The next day, however, brought important news from Antwerp. The city had surrendered, the Belgian army had made good its escape and was now retreating toward Ostend, closely followed by the enemy.

This news was related by a young orderly who met them as they entered the Hotel de Ville. They were also told that the commandant was very busy but would try to see them presently. This young Frenchman spoke English perfectly and was much excited by the morning's dispatches.

"This means that the war is headed our way at last!" he cried enthusiastically. "The Germans will make a dash to capture both Dunkirk and Calais, and already large bodies of reinforcements are on the way to defend these cities."

"English, or French?" asked Uncle John.

"This is French territory," was the embarrassed reply, "but we are glad to have our allies, the English, to support us. Their General French is now at Dunkirk, and it is probable the English will join the French and Belgians at that point."

"They didn't do much good at Antwerp, it seems," remarked Ajo.

"Ah, they were naval reserves, monsieur, and not much could be expected of them. But do not misunderstand me; I admire the English private—the fighting man—exceedingly. Were the officers as clever as their soldiers are brave, the English would be irresistible."

As this seemed a difficult subject to discuss, Uncle John asked the orderly if he knew of a good chauffeur to drive their ambulance—an able, careful man who might be depended upon in emergencies.

The orderly reflected.

"We have already impressed the best drivers," he said, "but it may be the general will consent to spare you one of them. Your work is so important that we must take good care of you."

But when they were admitted to the general they found him in a more impatient mood than before. He really could not undertake to direct Red Cross workers or advise them. They were needed everywhere; everywhere they would be welcome. And now, he regretted to state that he was very busy; if they had other business with the department, Captain Meroux would act as its representative.

Before accepting this dismissal Uncle John ventured to ask about a chauffeur. Rather brusquely the general stated that they could ill afford to spare one from the service. A desperate situation now faced the Allies in Flanders. Captain Meroux must take care of the Americans; doubtless he could find a driver for their ambulance— perhaps a Belgian.

But in the outer office the orderly smiled doubtfully.

A driver? To be sure; but such as he could furnish would not be of the slightest use to them. All the good chauffeurs had been impressed and the general was not disposed to let them have one.

"He mentioned a Belgian," suggested Uncle John.

"I know; but the Belgians in Calais are all fugitives, terror-stricken and unmanned." He grew thoughtful a moment and then continued:

36

"My advice would be to take your ship to Dunkirk. It is only a little way, through a good channel, and you will be as safe there as at Calais. For, if Dunkirk falls, Calais will fall with it. From there, moreover, the roads are better to Arras and Peronne, and it is there you stand the best chance of getting a clever Belgian chauffeur. If you wish—" he hesitated, looking at them keenly.

"Well, sir?"

"If you are really anxious to get to the firing line and do the most good, Dunkirk is your logical station. If you are merely seeking the notoriety of being charitably inclined, remain here."

They left the young man, reflecting upon his advice and gravely considering its value. They next visited one of the hospitals, where an overworked but friendly English surgeon volunteered a similar suggestion. Dunkirk, he declared, would give them better opportunities than Calais.

The remainder of the day they spent in getting whatever news had filtered into the city and vainly seeking a competent man for chauffeur. On the morning of October eleventh they left Calais and proceeded slowly along the buoyed channel that is the only means of approaching the port of Dunkirk by water. The coast line is too shallow to allow ships to enter from the open sea.

On their arrival at the Flemish city—twelve miles nearer the front than Calais—they found an entirely different atmosphere. No excitement, no terror was visible anywhere. The people quietly pursued their accustomed avocations and the city was as orderly as in normal times.

The town was full of Belgians, however, both soldiers and civilians, while French and British troops were arriving hourly in regiments and battalions. General French, the English commander in chief, had located his headquarters at a prominent hotel, and a brisk and businesslike air pervaded the place, with an entire lack of confusion. Most of the Belgians were reservists who were waiting to secure uniforms and arms. They crowded all the hotels, cafés and inns and seemed as merry and light-hearted as if no news of their king's defeat and precipitate retreat had arrived. Not until questioned would they discuss the war at all, yet every man was on the *qui vive*, expecting hourly to hear the roar of guns announcing the arrival of the fragment of the Belgian army that had escaped from Antwerp.

To-day the girls came ashore with the men of their party, all three wearing their Red Cross uniforms and caps, and it was almost pathetic to note the deference with which all those warriors—both bronzed and fair—removed their caps until the "angels of mercy" had passed them by.

They made the rounds of the hospitals, which were already crowded with wounded, and Gys stopped at one long enough to assist the French doctor in a delicate operation. Patsy stood by to watch this surgery, her face white and drawn, for this was her first experience of the sort; but Maud and Beth volunteered their services and were so calm and deft that Doctor Gys was well pleased with them.

CHAPTER VI

LITTLE MAURIE

It was nearly evening when the Americans finally returned to the quay, close to which the *Arabella* was moored. As they neared the place a great military automobile came tearing along, scattering pedestrians right and left, made a sudden swerve, caught a man who was not agile enough to escape and sent him spinning along the dock until he fell headlong, a crumpled heap.

"Ah, here is work for us!" exclaimed Doctor Gys, running forward to raise the man and examine his condition. The military car had not paused in its career and was well out of sight, but a throng of indignant civilians gathered around.

"There are no severe injuries, but he seems unconscious," reported Gys. "Let us get him aboard the ship."

The launch was waiting for them, and with the assistance of Jones, the doctor placed the injured man in the boat and he was taken to the ship and placed in one of the hospital berths.

"Our first patient is not a soldier, after all," remarked Patsy, a little disappointed. "I shall let Beth and Maud look after him."

"Well, he is wounded, all right," answered Ajo, "and without your kind permission Beth and Maud are already below, looking after him. I'm afraid he won't require their services long, poor fellow."

"Why didn't he get out of the way?" inquired Patsy with a shudder.

"Can't say. Preoccupied, perhaps. There wasn't much time to jump, anyhow. I suppose that car carried a messenger with important news, for it isn't like those officers to be reckless of the lives of citizens."

"No; they seem in perfect sympathy with the people," she returned. "I wonder what the news can be, Ajo."

For answer a wild whistling sounded overhead; a cry came from those ashore and the next instant there was a loud explosion. Everyone rushed to the side, where Captain Carg was standing, staring at the sky.

"What was it, Captain?" gasped Patsy.

Carg stroked his grizzled beard.

"A German bomb, Miss Patsy; but I think it did no damage."

"A bomb! Then the Germans are on us?"

"Not exactly. An aeroplane dropped the thing."

"Oh. Where is it?"

"The aeroplane? Pretty high up, I reckon," answered the captain. "I had a glimpse of it, for a moment; then it disappeared in the clouds."

"We must get our ambulances ashore," said Jones.

"No hurry, sir; plenty of time," asserted the captain. "I think I saw the airship floating north, so it isn't likely to bother us again just now."

"What place is north of us?" inquired the girl, trembling a little in spite of her efforts at control.

"I think it is Nieuport—or perhaps Dixmude," answered Carg. "I visited Belgium once, when I was a young man, but I cannot remember it very well. We're pretty close to the Belgian border, at Dunkirk."

"There's another!" cried Ajo, as a second whistling shriek sounded above them. This time the bomb fell into the sea and raised a small water-spout, some half mile distant. They could now see plainly a second huge aircraft circling above them; but this also took flight toward the north and presently disappeared.

Uncle John came hurrying on deck with an anxious face and together the group of Americans listened for more bombs; but that was all that came their way that night.

"Well," said Patsy, when she had recovered her equanimity, "we're at the front at last, Uncle. How do you like it?"

"I hadn't thought of bombs," he replied. "But we're in for it, and I suppose we'll have to take whatever comes."

Now came the doctor, supporting the injured man on one side while Maud Stanton held his opposite arm. Gys was smiling broadly—a rather ghastly expression.

"No bones broken, sir," he reported to Mr. Merrick. "Only a good shake-up and plenty of bruises. He can't be induced to stay in bed."

"Bed, when the Germans come?" exclaimed the invalid, scornfully, speaking in fair English. "It is absurd! We can sleep when we have driven them back to their dirty Faderland—we can sleep, then, and rest. Now, it is a crime to rest."

They looked at him curiously. He was a small man—almost a tiny man—lean and sinewy and with cheeks the color of bronze and eyes the hue of the sky. His head was quite bald at the top; his face wrinkled; he had a bushy mustache and a half-grown beard. His clothing was soiled, torn and neglected; but perhaps his accident accounted for much of its condition. His age might be anywhere from thirty to forty years. He looked alert and shrewd.

"You are Belgian?" said Uncle John.

He leaned against the rail, shaking off the doctor's support, as he replied:

"Yes, monsieur. Belgian born and American trained." There was a touch of pride in his voice. "It was in America that I made my fortune."

"Indeed."

"It is true. I was waiter in a New York restaurant for five years. Then I retired. I came back to Belgium. I married my wife. I bought land. It is near Ghent. I am, as you have guessed, a person of great importance."

"Ah; an officer, perhaps. Civil, or military?" inquired Ajo with mock deference.

"Of better rank than either. I am a citizen."

"Now, I like that spirit," said Uncle John approvingly. "What is your name, my good man?"

"Maurie, monsieur; Jakob Maurie. Perhaps you have met me—in New York."

"I do not remember it. But if you live in Ghent, why are you in Dunkirk?"

He cast an indignant glance at his questioner, but Uncle John's serene expression disarmed him.

"Monsieur is not here long?"

"We have just arrived."

"You cannot see Belgium from here. If you are there—in my country—you will find that the German is everywhere. I have my home at Brussels crushed by a shell which killed my baby girl. My land is devastate—my crop is taken to feed German horse and German thief. There is no home left. So my wife and my boy and girl I take away; I take them to Ostend, where I hope to get ship to England. At Ostend I am arrested by Germans. Not my wife and children; only myself. I am put in prison. For three weeks they keep me, and then I am put out. They push me into the street. No one apologize. I ask for my family. They laugh and turn away. I search everywhere for my wife. A friend whom I meet thinks she has gone to Ypres, for now no Belgian can take ship from Ostend to England. So I go to Ypres. The wandering people have all been sent to Nieuport and Dunkirk. Still I search. My wife is not in Nieuport. I come here, three days ago; I cannot find her in Dunkirk; she has vanished. Perhaps—but I will not trouble you with that. This is my story, ladies and gentlemen. Behold in me—a wealthy landowner of Liege—the outcast from home and country!"

"It is dreadful!" cried Patsy.

"It is fierce," said the man. "Only an American can understand the horror of that word."

"Your fate is surely a cruel one, Maurie," declared Mr. Merrick.

"Perhaps," ventured Beth, "we may help you to find your wife and children."

The Belgian seemed pleased with these expressions of sympathy. He straightened up, threw out his chest and bowed very low.

"That is my story," he repeated; "but you must know it is also the story of thousands of Belgians. Always I meet men searching for wives. Always I meet wives searching for husbands. Well! it is our fate—the fate of conquered Belgium."

Maud brought him a deck chair and made him sit down.

"You will stay here to-night," she said.

"That's right," said Dr. Gys. "He can't resume his search until morning, that's certain. Such a tumble as he had would have killed an ordinary man; but the fellow seems made of iron."

"To be a waiter—a good waiter—develops the muscles," said Maurie.

Ajo gave him a cigarette, which he accepted eagerly. After a few puffs he said:

"I heard the German bombs. That means the enemy grows insolent. First they try to frighten us with bombs, then they attack."

"How far away do you think the Germans are?" asked Beth.

"Nieuport les Bains. But they will get no nearer."

"No?"

"Surely not, mamselle. Our soldiers are there, awaiting them. Our soldiers, and the French."

"And you think the enemy cannot capture Dunkirk?" inquired Jones.

"Dunkirk! The Germans capture Dunkirk? It is impossible."

"Why impossible?"

"Dunkirk is fortified; it is the entrance to Calais, to Dover and London. Look you, m'sieur; we cannot afford to lose this place. We cannot afford to lose even Nieuport, which is our last stand on Belgian soil. Therefore, the Germans cannot take it, for there are still too many of us to kill before Kitchener comes to save us." He spoke thoughtfully, between puffs of his cigarette, and added: "But of course, if the great English army does not come, and they kill us all, then it will not matter in the least what becomes of our country."

Maurie's assertion did not wholly reassure them. The little Belgian was too bombastic to win their confidence in his judgment. Yet Jones declared that Maurie doubtless knew the country better than anyone they had yet met and the doctor likewise defended his patient. Indeed, Gys seemed to have taken quite a fancy to the little man and long after the others had retired for the night he sat on deck talking with the Belgian and getting his views of the war.

"You say you had land at Ghent?" he once asked.

"It is true, Doctor."

"But afterward you said Brussels."

Maurie was not at all confused.

"Ah; I may have done so. You see, I traded my property."

"And, if I am not mistaken, you spoke of a home at Liege."

Maurie looked at him reproachfully.

"Is there not much land in Belgium?" he demanded; "and is a rich man confined to one home? Liege was my summer home; in the winter I removed to Antwerp."

"You said Ghent."

"Ghent it was, Doctor. Misfortune has dulled my brain. I am not the man I was," he added with a sigh.

"Nevertheless," said Gys, "you still possess the qualities of a good waiter. Whatever happens here, Maurie, you can always go back to America."

CHAPTER VII

ON THE FIRING LINE

Next morning they were all wakened at an early hour by the roar of artillery, dimly heard in the distance. The party aboard the *Arabella* quickly assembled on deck, where little Maurie was found leaning over the rail.

"They're at it," he remarked, wagging his head. "The Germans are at Nieuport, now, and some of them are over against Pervyse. I hear sounds from Dixmude, too; the rattle of machine guns. It will be a grand battle, this! I wonder if our Albert is there."

"Who is he?" asked Patsy.

"The king. They told me yesterday he had escaped."

"We must get the ambulances out at once," said Beth.

"I'll attend to that," replied Uncle John, partaking of the general excitement. "Warp up to the dock, Captain Carg, and I'll get some of those men to help us swing the cars over the side."

"How about a chauffeur?" asked Dr. Gys, who was already bringing out bandages and supplies for the ambulances.

"If we can't find a man, I'll drive you myself," declared Ajo.

"But you don't know the country."

Gys turned to the little Belgian.

"Can't you find us a driver?" he asked. "We want a steady, competent man to run our ambulance."

"Where are you going?" asked Maurie.

"To the firing line."

"Good. I will drive you myself."

"You? Do you understand a car?"

"I am an expert, monsieur."

"A waiter in a restaurant?"

"Pah! That was five years ago. I will show you. I can drive any car ever made—and I know every inch of the way."

"Then you're our man," exclaimed Mr. Merrick, much relieved.

As the yacht swung slowly alongside the dock the Belgian said:

"While you get ready, I will go ashore for news. When I come back—very quick—then I will know everything."

Before he ran down the ladder Patsy clasped around his arm a band bearing the insignia of the Red Cross. He watched her approvingly, with little amused chuckles, and then quickly disappeared in the direction of the town.

"He doesn't seem injured in the least by his accident," said the girl, looking after him as he darted along.

"No," returned Gys; "he is one of those fellows who must be ripped to pieces before they can feel anything. But let us thank heaven he can drive a car."

Mr. Merrick had no difficulty in getting all the assistance required to lower the two ambulances to the dock. They had already been set up and put in order, so the moment they were landed they were ready for use.

A few surgical supplies were added by Dr. Gys and then they looked around for the Belgian. Although scarce an hour had elapsed since he departed, he came running back just as he was needed, puffing a little through haste, his eyes shining with enthusiasm.

"Albert is there!" he cried. "The king and his army are at Nieuport. They will open the dykes and flood all the country but the main road, and then we can hold the enemy in check. They will fight, those Germans, but they cannot advance, for we will defend the road and the sand dunes."

"Aren't they fighting now?" asked Jones.

"Oh, yes, some of the big guns are spitting, but what is that? A few will fall, but we have yet thousands to face the German horde."

"Let us start at once," pleaded Maud.

Maurie began to examine the big ambulance. He was spry as a cat. In ten minutes he knew all that was under the hood, had tested the levers, looked at the oil and gasoline supply and started the motor.

"I'll sit beside you to help in case of emergency," said Ajo, taking his place. Dr. Gys, Dr. Kelsey and the three girls sat inside. Patsy had implored Uncle John not to go on this preliminary expedition and he had hesitated until the last moment; but the temptation was too strong to resist and even as the wheels started to revolve he sprang in and closed the door behind him.

"You are my girls," he said, "and wherever you go, I'll tag along."

Maurie drove straight into the city and to the north gate, Jones clanging the bell as they swept along. Every vehicle gave them the right of way and now and then a cheer greeted the glittering new Red Cross ambulance, which bore above its radiator a tiny, fluttering American flag.

They were not stopped at the gate, for although strict orders had been issued to allow no one to leave Dunkirk, the officer in charge realized the sacred mission of the Americans and merely doffed his cap in salutation as the car flashed by.

The road to Furnes was fairly clear, but as they entered that town they found the streets cluttered with troops, military automobiles, supply wagons, artillery, ammunition trucks and bicycles. The boy clanged his bell continuously and as if by magic the way opened before the Red Cross and cheers followed them on their way.

The eyes of the little Belgian were sparkling like jewels; his hands on the steering wheel were steady as a rock; he drove with skill and judgment. Just now the road demanded skill, for a stream of refugees was coming toward them from Nieuport and a stream of military motors, bicycles and wagons, with now and then a horseman, flowed toward the front. A mile or two beyond Furnes they came upon a wounded soldier, one leg bandaged and stained with blood while he hobbled along leaning upon the shoulder of a comrade whose left arm hung helpless.

Maurie drew up sharply and Beth sprang out and approached the soldiers.

"Get inside," she said in French.

"No," replied one, smiling; "we are doing nicely, thank you. Hurry forward, for they need you there."

"Who dressed your wounds?" she inquired.

"The Red Cross. There are many there, hard at work; but more are needed. Hurry forward, for some of our boys did not get off as lightly as we."

She jumped into the ambulance and away it dashed, but progress became slower presently. The road was broad and high; great hillocks of sand—the Dunes—lay between it and the ocean; on the other side the water from the opened dykes was already turning the fields into an inland sea. In some places it lapped the edges of the embankment that formed the roadway.

Approaching Nieuport, they discovered the Dunes to be full of soldiers, who had dug pits behind the sandy hillocks for protection, and in them planted the dog-artillery and one or two large machine guns. These were trained on the distant line of Germans, who were also entrenching themselves. All along the edge of the village the big guns were in action and there was a constant interchange of shot and shell from both sides.

As Maurie dodged among the houses with the big car a shell descended some two hundred yards to the left of them, exploded with a crash and sent a shower of brick and splinters high into the air. A little way farther on the ruins of a house completely blocked the street and they were obliged to turn back and seek another passage. Thus partially skirting the town they at last left the houses behind them and approached the firing line, halting scarcely a quarter of a mile distant from the actual conflict.

As far as the eye could reach, from Nieuport to the sea at the left, and on toward Ypres at the right of them, the line of Belgians, French and British steadily faced the foe. Close to where they halted the ambulance stood a detachment that had lately retired from the line, their places having been taken by reserves. One of the officers told Mr. Merrick that they had been facing bullets since daybreak and the men seemed almost exhausted. Their faces were blackened by dust and powder and their uniforms torn and disordered; many stood without caps or coats despite the chill in the air. And yet these fellows were laughing together and chatting as pleasantly as children just released from school. Even those who had wounds made light of their hurts. Clouds of smoke hovered low in the air; the firing was incessant.

Our girls were thrilled by this spectacle as they had never been thrilled before—perhaps never might be again. While they still kept their seats, Maurie started with a sudden jerk, made a sharp turn and ran the ambulance across a ridge of solid earth that seemed to be the only one of such character amongst all that waste of sand. It brought them somewhat closer to the line but their driver drew up behind a great dune that afforded them considerable protection.

Fifty yards away was another ambulance with its wheels buried to the hubs in the loose sand. Red Cross nurses and men wearing the emblem on their arms and caps were passing here and there, assisting the injured with "first aid," temporarily bandaging heads, arms and legs or carrying to the rear upon a stretcher a more seriously injured man. Most of this corps were French; a few were English; some were Belgian. Our friends were the only Americans on the field.

Uncle John's face was very grave as he alighted in the wake of his girls, who paid no attention to the fighting but at once ran to assist some of the wounded who came staggering toward the ambulance, some even creeping painfully on hands and knees. In all Mr.

Merrick's conceptions of the important mission they had undertaken, nothing like the nature of this desperate conflict had even dawned upon him. He had known that the Red Cross was respected by all belligerents, and that knowledge had led him to feel that his girls would be fairly safe; but never had he counted on spent bullets, stray shells or the mad rush of a charge.

"Very good!" cried Maurie briskly. "Here we see what no one else can see. The Red Cross is a fine passport to the grand stand of war."

"Come with me—quick!" shouted Ajo, his voice sounding shrill through the din. "I saw a fellow knocked out—there—over yonder!"

As he spoke he grabbed a stretcher and ran forward, Maurie following at his heels. Uncle John saw the smoke swallow them up, saw Beth and Maud each busy with lint, plasters and bandages, saw Patsy supporting a tall, grizzled warrior who came limping toward the car. Then he turned and saw Doctor Gys, crouching low against the protecting sand, his disfigured face working convulsively and every limb trembling as with an ague.

CHAPTER VIII

THE COWARD

"Great heavens!" gasped Mr. Merrick, running toward the doctor. "Are you hit?"

Gys looked up at him appealingly and nodded.

"Where did it strike you? Was it a bullet—or what?"

The doctor wrung his hands, moaning pitifully. Uncle John bent over him.

"Tell me," he said. "Tell me, Gys!"

"I—I'm scared, sir—s-s-scared stiff. It's that yellow s-s-s-streak in me; I—I—can't help it, sir." Then he collapsed, crouching lifelessly close to the sand.

Uncle John was amazed. He drew back with such an expression of scorn that Gys, lying with face upward, rolled over to hide his own features in the sand. But his form continued to twist and shake convulsively.

Patsy came up with her soldier, whose gaudy uniform proclaimed him an officer. He had a rugged, worn face, gray hair and mustache, stern eyes. His left side was torn and bleeding where a piece of shell had raked him from shoulder to knee. No moan did he utter as Mr. Merrick and the girl assisted him to one of the swinging beds, and then Patsy, with white, set face but steady hands, began at once to cut away the clothing and get at the wound. This was her first practical experience and she meant to prove her mettle or perish in the attempt.

Uncle John skipped over to the sand bank and clutched Gys savagely by the collar.

"Get up!" he commanded. "Here's a man desperately wounded, who needs your best skill—and at once."

Gys pulled himself free and sat up, seeming dazed for the moment. Then he rubbed his head briskly with both hands, collected his nerve and slowly rose to his feet. He cast fearful glances at the firing line, but the demand for his surgical skill was a talisman that for a time enabled him to conquer his terror. With frightened backward glances he ran to the ambulance and made a dive into it as if a pack of wolves was at his heels.

Safely inside, one glance at the wounded man caused Gys to stiffen suddenly. He became steady and alert and noting that Patsy had now bared a portion of the gaping wound the doctor seized a thermos flask of hot water and in a moment was removing the clotted blood in a deft and intelligent manner.

Now came Jones and Maurie bearing the man they had picked up. As they set the stretcher down, Uncle John came over.

"Shall we put him inside?" asked Mr. Merrick.

"No use, I think," panted the Belgian.

"Where's the doctor?" asked Ajo.

Kelsey, who had been busy elsewhere, now approached and looked at the soldier on the stretcher.

"The man is dead," he said. "He doesn't need us now."

"Off with him, then!" cried Maurie, and they laid the poor fellow upon the sand and covered him with a cloth. "Come, then," urged the little chauffeur, excitedly, "lots more out there are still alive. We get one quick."

They left in a run in one direction while Kelsey, who had come to the ambulance for supplies, went another way. Mr. Merrick looked around for the other two girls. Only Maud Stanton was visible through the smoky haze. Uncle John approached her just as a shell dropped into the sand not fifty feet away. It did not explode but plowed a deep furrow and sent a shower of sand in every direction.

Maud had just finished dressing a bullet wound in the arm of a young soldier who smiled as he watched her. Then, as she finished the work, he bowed low, muttered his thanks, and catching up his gun rushed back into the fray. It was a flesh wound and until it grew more painful he could still fight.

"Where are the Germans?" asked Uncle John. "I haven't seen one yet."

As he spoke a great cheer rose from a thousand throats. The line before them wavered an instant and then rushed forward and disappeared in the smoke of battle.

"Is it a charge, do you think?" asked Maud, as they stood peering into the haze.

"I—I don't know," he stammered. "This is so—so bewildering—that it all seems like a dream. Where's Beth?"

"I don't know."

"Are you looking for a young lady—a nurse?" asked a voice beside them. "She's over yonder," he swung one arm toward the distant sand dunes. The other was in a sling. "She has just given me first aid and sent me to the rear—God bless her!" Then he trailed on, a British Tommy Atkins, while with one accord Maud and Uncle John moved in the direction he had indicated.

"She mustn't be so reckless," said Beth's uncle, nervously. "It's bad enough back here, but every step nearer the firing line doubles the danger."

"I do not agree with you, sir," answered Maud quietly. "A man was killed not two paces from me, a little while ago."

He shuddered and wiped the sweat from his forehead with a handkerchief, but made no reply. They climbed another line of dunes and in the hollow beyond came upon several fallen soldiers, one of whom was moaning with pain. Maud ran to kneel beside him and in a twinkling had her hypodermic needle in his arm.

"Bear it bravely," she said in French. "The pain will stop in a few minutes and then I'll come and look after you."

He nodded gratefully, still moaning, and she hurried to rejoin Mr. Merrick.

"Beth must be in the next hollow," said Uncle John as she overtook him, and his voice betrayed his nervous tension. "I do wish you girls would not be so reckless."

Yes; they found her in the next hollow, where several men were grouped about her. She was dressing the shattered hand of a soldier, while two or three others were patiently awaiting her services. Just beside her a sweet-faced Sister of Mercy was bending over a dying man, comforting him with her prayers. Over the ridge of sand could be heard the "ping" of small arms mingled with the hoarse roar of machine guns. Another great shout—long and enthusiastic—was borne to their ears.

"That is good," said a tall man standing in the group about Beth; "I think, from the sound, we have captured their guns."

"I'm sure of it, your Majesty," replied the one whom Beth was attending. "There; that will do for the present. I thank you. And now, let us get forward."

As they ran toward the firing Uncle John exclaimed:

"His Majesty! I wonder who they are?"

"That," said a private soldier, an accent of pride in his voice, "is our Albert."

"The king?"

"Yes, monsieur; he is the tall one. The other is General Mays. I'm sure we have driven the Germans back, and that is lucky, for before our charge they had come too close for comfort."

"The king gave me a ring," said Beth, displaying it. "He seemed glad I was here to help his soldiers, but warned me to keep further away from the line. King Albert speaks English perfectly and told me he loves America better than any other country except his own."

"He has traveled in your country," explained the soldier. "But then, our Albert has traveled everywhere—before he was king."

Betwixt them Maud and Beth quickly applied first aid to the others in the group and then Uncle John said:

"Let us take the king's advice and get back to the ambulance. We left only Patsy and Dr. Gys there and I'm sure you girls will be needed."

On their return they came upon a man sitting in a hollow and calmly leaning against a bank of sand, smoking a cigarette. He wore a gray uniform.

"Ah, a German!" exclaimed Maud. She ran up to him and asked: "Are you hurt?"

He glanced at her uniform, nodded, and pointed to his left foot. It had nearly all been torn away below the ankle. A handkerchief was twisted about the leg, forming a rude tourniquet just above the wound, and this had served to stay the flow of blood.

"Run quickly for the stretcher," said Maud to Uncle John. "I will stay with him until your return."

Without a word he hurried away, Beth following. They found, on reaching the ambulance, that Maurie and Jones had been busy. Five of the swinging beds were already occupied.

"Save the other one," said Beth. "Maud has found a German." Then she hurried to assist Patsy, as the two doctors had their hands full.

Jones and Maurie started away with the stretcher, Uncle John guiding them to the dunes where Maud was waiting, and presently they had the wounded German comfortably laid in the last bed.

"Now, then, back to the ship," said Gys. "We have in our care two lives, at least, that can only be saved by prompt operations."

Maurie got into the driver's seat.

"Careful, now!" cautioned Jones, beside him.

"Of course," replied the Belgian, starting the motor; "there are many sores inside. But if they get a jolt, now and then, it will serve to remind them that they are suffering for their country."

He began to back up, for the sand ahead was too deep for a turn, and the way he managed the huge car along that narrow ridge aroused the admiration of Ajo, who alone was able to witness the marvelous performance. Slowly, with many turns, they backed to the road, where Maurie swung the ambulance around and then stopped with a jerk that drew several groans from the interior of the car.

"What's wrong?" asked Mr. Merrick, sticking his head from a window.

"We nearly ran over a man," answered Jones, climbing down from his seat. "Our front wheels are right against him, but Maurie stopped in time."

Lying flat upon his face, diagonally across the roadway, was the form of a man in the blue-and-red uniform of the Belgian army. Maurie backed the ambulance a yard or so as Maud sprang out and knelt beside the prostrate form.

The firing, which had lulled for a few minutes, suddenly redoubled in fury. There rose a wild, exultant shout, gradually drawing nearer.

"Quick!" shouted Gys, trembling and wringing his hands. "The Germans are charging. Drive on, man—drive on!"

But Maurie never moved.

"The Germans are charging, sure enough," he answered, as the line of retreating Belgians became visible. "But they must stop here, for we've blocked the road."

All eyes but those of Maud were now turned upon the fray, which was practically a hand to hand conflict. Nearer and nearer came the confused mass of warriors and then, scarce a hundred yards away, it halted and the Belgians stood firm.

"He isn't dead," said Maud, coming to the car. "Help me to put him inside."

"There is no room," protested Gys.

The girl looked at him scornfully.

"We will make room," she replied.

A bullet shattered a pane of glass just beside the crouching doctor, but passed on through an open window without injuring anyone. In fact, bullets were singing around them with a freedom that made others than Dr. Gys nervous. It was chubby little Uncle John who helped Jones carry the wounded man to the ambulance, where they managed to stretch him upon the floor. This arrangement sent Patsy to the front seat outside, with Maurie and Ajo, although her uncle strongly protested that she had no right to expose her precious life so wantonly.

There was little time for argument, however. Even as the girl was climbing to her seat the line of Belgians broke and came pouring toward them. Maurie was prompt in starting the car and the next moment the ambulance was rolling swiftly along the smooth highway in the direction of Dunkirk and the sounds of fray grew faint behind them.

CHAPTER IX

COURAGE, OR PHILOSOPHY?

"I never realized," said Maud, delightedly, "what a strictly modern, professional hospital ship Uncle John has made of this, until we put it to practical use. I am sure it is better than those makeshifts we observed at Calais, and more comfortable than those crowded hospitals on land. Every convenience is at our disposal and if our patients do not recover rapidly it will be because their condition is desperate."

She had just come on deck after a long and trying session in assisting Doctors Gys and Kelsey to care for the injured, a session during which Beth and Patsy had also stood nobly to their gruesome task. There were eleven wounded, altogether, in their care, and although some of these were in a critical condition the doctors had insisted that the nurses needed rest.

"It is Dr. Gys who deserves credit for fitting the ship," replied Mr. Merrick, modestly, to Maud's enthusiastic comment, "and Ajo is responsible for the ship itself, which seems admirably suited to our purpose. By the way, how is Gys behaving now? Is he still shaking with fear?"

"No, he seems to have recovered his nerve. Isn't it a terrible affliction?"

"Cowardice? Well, my dear, it is certainly an unusual affliction in this country and in these times. I have been amazed to-day at the courage I have witnessed. These Belgians are certainly a brave lot."

"But no braver than the German we brought with us," replied Maud thoughtfully. "One would almost think he had no sensation, yet he must be suffering terribly. The doctor will amputate the remnants of his foot in an hour or so, but the man positively refuses to take an anaesthetic."

"Does he speak English or French?"

"No; only German. But Captain Carg understands German and so he has been acting as our interpreter."

"How about the Belgian we picked up on the road?"

"He hasn't recovered consciousness yet. He is wounded in the back and in trying to get to the rear became insensible from loss of blood."

"From what I saw I wouldn't suppose any Belgian could be wounded in the back," remarked Uncle John doubtfully.

"It was a shell," she said, "and perhaps exploded behind him. It's a bad wound, Dr. Gys says, but if he regains strength he may recover."

During this conversation Patsy Doyle was lying in her stateroom below and crying bitterly, while her cousin Beth strove to soothe her. All unused to such horrors as she had witnessed that day, the girl had managed to retain her nerve by sheer force of will until the Red Cross party had returned to the ship and extended first aid to the wounded; but the moment Dr. Gys dismissed her she broke down completely.

Beth was no more accustomed to bloodshed than her cousin, but she had anticipated such scenes as they had witnessed, inasmuch as her year of training as nurse had prepared her for them. She had also been a close student of the daily press and from her reading had gleaned a knowledge of the terrible havoc wrought by this great war. Had Patsy not given way, perhaps Beth might have done so herself, and really it was Maud Stanton who bore the ordeal with the most composure.

After a half hour on deck Maud returned to the hospital section quite refreshed, and proceeded to care for the patients. She alone assisted Gys and Kelsey to amputate the German's foot, an operation the man bore splendidly, quite unaware, however, that they had applied local anaesthetics to dull the pain. Dr. Gys was a remarkably skillful surgeon and he gave himself no rest until every one of the eleven had received such attention as his wounds demanded. Even Kelsey felt the strain by that time and as Maud expressed her intention of remaining to minister to the wants of the crippled soldiers, the two doctors went on deck for a smoke and a brief relaxation.

By this time Beth had quieted Patsy, mainly by letting her have her cry out, and now brought her on deck to join the others and get the fresh air. So quickly had events followed one another on this fateful day that it was now only four o'clock in the afternoon. None of them had thought of luncheon, so the ship's steward now brought tea and sandwiches to those congregated on deck.

As they sat together in a group, drinking tea and discussing the exciting events of the day, little Maurie came sauntering toward them and removed his cap.

"Your pardon," said he, "but—are the wounded all cared for?"

"As well as we are able to care for them at present," answered Beth. "And let me thank you, Jakob Maurie—let us all thank you—for the noble work you did for us to-day."

"Pah! it was nothing," said he, shifting from one foot to another. "I enjoyed it, mamselle. It was such fun to dive into the battle and pull out the wounded. It helped them, you see, and it gave us a grand excitement. Otherwise, had I not gone with you, I would be as ignorant as all in Dunkirk still are, for the poor people do not yet know what has happened at the front."

"We hardly know ourselves what has happened," said Uncle John. "We can hear the boom of guns yet, even at this distance, and we left the battle line flowing back and forth like the waves of the ocean. Have a cup of tea, Maurie?"

The man hesitated.

"I do not like to disturb anyone," he said slowly, "but if one of the young ladies is disengaged I would be grateful if she looks at my arm."

"Your arm!" exclaimed Beth, regarding him wonderingly as he stood before her.

Maurie smiled.

"It is hardly worth mentioning, mamselle, but a bullet—"

"Take off your coat," she commanded, rising from her seat to assist him.

Maurie complied. His shirt was stained with blood. Beth drew out her scissors and cut away the sleeve of his left arm. A bullet had passed directly through the flesh, but without harming bone or muscle.

"Why didn't you tell us before?" she asked reproachfully.

"It amounted to so little, beside the other hurts you had to attend," he answered. "I am shamed, mamselle, that I came to you at all. A little water and a cloth will make it all right."

Patsy had already gone for the water and in a few minutes Beth was deftly cleansing the wound.

"How did it happen, Maurie?" asked Jones. "I was with you most of the time and noticed nothing wrong. Besides, you said nothing about it."

"It was on the road, just as we picked up that fallen soldier with the hole in his back. The fight jumped toward us pretty quick, you remember, and while I sat at the wheel the bullet came. I knew when it hit me, but I also knew I could move my arm, so what did it matter? I told myself to wait till we got to the ship. Had we stayed there longer, we might all have stopped bullets—and some bullets might have stopped us." He grinned, as if the aphorism amused him, and added: "To know when to run is the perfection of courage."

"Does it hurt?" asked Uncle John, as Beth applied the lint and began winding the bandage.

"It reminds me it is there, monsieur; but I will be ready for another trip to-morrow. Thank you, mamselle. Instead of the tea, I would like a little brandy."

"Give him some in the tea," suggested Gys, noting that Maurie swayed a little. "Sit down, man, and be comfortable. That's it. I'd give a million dollars for your nerve."

"Have you so much money?" asked Maurie.

"No."

"Then I cannot see that you lack nerve," said the little Belgian thoughtfully. "I was watching you to-day, M'sieur Doctor, and I believe what you lack is courage."

Gys stared so hard at him with the one good eye that even Maurie became embarrassed and turned away his head. Sipping his tea and brandy he presently resumed, in a casual tone:

"Never have I indulged in work of more interest than this. We go into the thick of the fight, yet are we safe from harm. We do good to both sides, because the men who do the fighting are not to blame for the war, at all. The leaders of politics say to the generals: 'We have declared war; go and fight.' The generals say to the soldiers: 'We are told to fight, so come on. We do not know why, but it is our duty, because it is our profession. So go and die, or get shot to pieces, or lose some arms and legs, as it may happen.' The business of the soldiers is to obey; they must back up the policies of their country, right or wrong. But do those who send them into danger ever get hurt? Not to the naked eye."

"Why, you're quite a philosopher, Maurie," said Patsy.

"It is true," agreed the Belgian. "But philosophy is like courage—easy to assume. We strut and talk big; we call the politicians sharks, the soldiers fools; but does it do any good? The war will go on; the enemy will destroy our homes, separate our families, take away our bread and leave us to starve; but we have the privilege to philosophize, if we like. For myself, I thank them for nothing!"

"I suppose you grieve continually for your wife," said Patsy.

"Not so much that, mamselle, but I know she is grieving for me," he replied.

"As soon as we find time," continued the girl, "we intend to search for your wife and children. I am sure we can find them for you."

Maurie moved uneasily in his chair.

"I beg you to take no trouble on my account," said he. "With the Red Cross you have great work to accomplish. What is the despair of one poor Walloon to you?"

"It is a great deal to us, Maurie," returned the girl, earnestly. "You have been a friend in need; without you we could not have made our dash to the front to-day. We shall try to repay you by finding your wife."

He was silent, but his troubled look told of busy thoughts.

"What does she look like?" inquired Beth. "Have you her photograph?"

"No; she would not make a good picture, mamselle," he answered with a sigh. "Clarette is large; she is fat; she has a way of scowling when one does not bring in more wood than the fire can eat up; and she is very religious."

"With that description I am sure we can find her," cried Patsy enthusiastically.

He seemed disturbed.

"If you please," said he plaintively, "Clarette is quite able to take care of herself. She has a strong will."

"But if you know she is safe it will relieve your anxiety," suggested Beth. "You told us yesterday you had been searching everywhere for her."

"If I said everywhere, I was wrong, for poor Clarette must be somewhere. And since yesterday I have been thinking with more deliberation, and I have decided," he added, his tone becoming confidential, "that it is better I do not find Clarette just now. It might destroy my usefulness to the Red Cross."

"But your children!" protested Patsy. "Surely you cannot rest at ease with your two dear children wandering about, in constant danger."

"To be frank, mamselle," said he, "they are not my children. I had a baby, but it was killed, as I told you. The boy and girl I have mentioned were born when Clarette was the wife of another man—a blacksmith at Dinant—who had a sad habit of beating her."

"But you love the little ones, I am sure."

He shook his head.

"They have somewhat the temper of their father, the blacksmith. I took them when I took Clarette—just as I took the silver spoons and the checkered tablespread she brought with her—but now that a cruel fate has separated me from the children, perhaps it is all for the best."

The doctor gave a snort of disgust, while Ajo smiled. The girls were too astonished to pursue the conversation, but now realized that Maurie's private affairs did not require their good offices to untangle. Uncle John was quite amused at the Belgian's confession and was the only one to reply.

"Fate often seems cruel when she is in her happiest mood," said he. "Perhaps, Maurie, your Clarette will come to you without your seeking her, for all Belgium seems headed toward France just now. What do you think? Will the Germans capture Dunkirk?"

The man brightened visibly at this turn in the conversation.

"Not to-day, sir; not for days to come," he replied. "The French cannot afford to lose Dunkirk, and by to-morrow they will pour an irresistible horde against the German invader. If we stay here, we are sure to remain in the rear of the firing line."

CHAPTER X

THE WAR'S VICTIMS

While the others were conversing on deck Maud Stanton was ministering to the maimed victims of the war's cruelty, who tossed and moaned below. The main cabin and its accompanying staterooms had been fitted with all the conveniences of a modern hospital. Twenty-two could easily be accommodated in the rooms and a dozen more in the cabin, so that the eleven now in their charge were easily cared for. Of these, only three had been seriously injured. One was the German, who, however, was now sleeping soundly under the influence of the soothing potion that followed his operation. The man's calmness and iron nerve indicated that he would make a rapid recovery. Another was the young Belgian soldier picked up in the roadway near the firing line, who had been shot in the back and had not yet recovered consciousness. Dr. Gys had removed several bits of exploded shell and dressed the wound, shaking his head discouragingly. But since the young man was still breathing, with a fairly regular respiration, no attempt was made to restore him to his senses.

The third seriously injured was a French sergeant whose body was literally riddled with shrapnel. A brief examination had convinced Gys that the case was hopeless.

"He may live until morning," was the doctor's report as he calmly looked down upon the moaning sergeant, "but no longer. Meanwhile, we must prevent his suffering."

This he accomplished by means of powerful drugs. The soldier soon lay in a stupor, awaiting the end, and nothing more could be done for him.

Of the others, two Belgians with bandaged heads were playing a quiet game of écarté in a corner of the cabin, while another with a slight wound in his leg was stretched upon a couch, reading a book. A young French officer who had lost three fingers of his hand was cheerfully conversing with a comrade whose scalp had been torn by a bullet and who declared that in two days he would return to the front. The others Maud found asleep in their berths or lying quietly to ease their pain. It was remarkable, however, how little suffering was caused these men by flesh wounds, once they were properly dressed and the patients made comfortable with food and warmth and the assurance of proper care.

So it was that Maud found her duties not at all arduous this evening. Indeed, the sympathy she felt for these brave men was so strong that it wearied her more than the actual work of nursing them. A sip of water here, a cold compress there, the administration of medicines to keep down or prevent fever, little attentions of this character were all that were required. Speaking French fluently, she was able to converse with all those under her charge and all seemed eager to relate to their beautiful nurse their experiences, hopes and griefs. Soon she realized she was beginning to learn more of the true nature of war than she had ever gleaned from the correspondents of the newspapers.

When dinner was served in the forward cabin Beth relieved Maud and after the evening meal Dr. Gys made another inspection of his patients. All seemed doing well except the young Belgian. The condition of the French sergeant was still unchanged. Some of those with minor injuries were ordered on deck for a breath of fresh air.

Patsy relieved Beth at midnight and Maud came on duty again at six o'clock, having had several hours of refreshing sleep. She found Patsy trembling with nervousness, for the sergeant had passed away an hour previous and the horror of the event had quite upset the girl.

"Oh, it is all so unnecessary!" she wailed as she threw herself into Maud's arms.

"We must steel ourselves to such things, dear," said Maud, soothing her, "for they will be of frequent occurrence, I fear. And we must be grateful and glad that we were able to relieve the poor man's anguish and secure for him a peaceful end."

"I know," answered Patsy with a little sob, "but it's so dreadful. Oh, what a cruel, hateful thing war is!"

From papers found on the sergeant Uncle John was able to notify his relatives of his fate. His home was in a little village not fifty miles away and during the day a brother arrived to take charge of the remains and convey them to their last resting place.

The following morning Captain Carg was notified by the authorities to withdraw the *Arabella* to an anchorage farther out in the bay, and thereafter it became necessary to use the two launches for intercourse between the ship and the city. Continuous cannonading could be heard from the direction of Nieuport, Dixmude and Ypres, and it was evident that the battle had doubled in intensity at all points, owing to heavy reinforcements being added to both sides. But, as Maurie had predicted, the Allies were able to hold the foe at bay and keep them from advancing a step farther.

Uncle John had not been at all satisfied with that first day's experience at the front. He firmly believed it was unwise, to the verge of rashness, to allow the girls to place themselves in so dangerous a position. During a serious consultation with Jones, Kelsey, Captain Carg and Dr. Gys, the men agreed upon a better plan of procedure.

"The three nurses have plenty to do in attending to the patients in our hospital," said Gys, "and when the ship has its full quota of wounded they will need assistance or they will break down under the strain. Our young ladies are different from the professional nurses; they are so keenly sensitive that they suffer from sympathy with every patient that comes under their care."

"I do not favor their leaving the ship," remarked Dr. Kelsey, the mate. "There seems to be plenty of field workers at the front, supplied by the governments whose troops are fighting."

"Therefore," added Jones, "we men must assume the duty of driving the ambulances and bringing back the wounded we are able to pick up. As Maurie is too stiff from his wound to drive to-day, I shall undertake the job myself. I know the way, now, and am confident I shall get along nicely. Who will go with me?"

"I will, of course," replied Kelsey quietly.

"Doctor Gys will be needed on the ship," asserted Uncle John.

"Yes, it will be best to leave me here," said Gys. "I'm too great a coward to go near the firing line again. It destroys my usefulness, and Kelsey can administer first aid as well as I."

"In that case, I think I shall take the small ambulance to-day," decided Ajo. "With Dr. Kelsey and one of the sailors we shall manage very well."

A launch took them ashore, where the ambulances stood upon the dock. Maurie had admitted his inability to drive, but asked to be allowed to go into the town. So he left the ship with the others and disappeared for the day.

Ajo took the same route he had covered before, in the direction of Nieuport, but could not get within five miles of the town, which was now held by the Germans. From Furnes to the front the roads were packed with reinforcements and wagon trains bearing ammunition and supplies, and further progress with the ambulance was impossible.

However, a constant stream of wounded flowed to the rear, some with first aid bandages covering their injuries, others as yet uncared for. Kelsey chose those whom he considered most in need of surgical care or skillful nursing, and by noon the ambulance was filled to overflowing. It was Jones who advised taking none of the fatally injured, as the army surgeons paid especial attention to these. The Americans could be of most practical use, the boy considered, by taking in charge such as had a chance to recover. So nine more patients were added to the ship's colony on this occasion, all being delivered to the care of Dr. Gys without accident or delay—a fact that rendered Ajo quite proud of his skillful driving.

While the ambulance was away the girls quietly passed from berth to berth, encouraging and caring for their wounded. It was surprising how interested they became in the personality of these soldiers, for each man was distinctive either in individuality or the character of his injury, and most of them were eager to chat with their nurses and anxious for news of the battle.

During the morning the young Belgian who had lain until now in a stupor, recovered consciousness. He had moaned once or twice, drawing Maud to his side, but hearing a different sound from him she approached the berth where he lay, to find his eyes wide open. Gradually he turned them upon his nurse, as if feeling her presence, and after a moment of observation he sighed and then smiled wanly.

"Still on earth?" he said in French.

"I am so glad," she replied. "You have been in dreamland a long time."

He tried to move and it brought a moan to his lips.

"Don't stir," she counseled warningly; "you are badly wounded."

He was silent for a time, staring at the ceiling. She held some water to his lips and he drank eagerly. Finally he said in a faint voice:

"I remember, now. I had turned to reload and it hit me in the back. A bullet, mademoiselle?"

"Part of a shell."

"Ah, I understand.... I tried to get to the rear. The pain was terrible. No one seemed to notice me. At last I fell, and—then I slept. I thought it was the end."

She bathed his forehead, saying:

"You must not talk any more at present. Here comes the doctor to see you."

Gys, busy in the cabin, had heard their voices and now came to look at his most interesting patient. The soldier seemed about twenty years of age; he was rather handsome, with expressive eyes and features bearing the stamp of culture. Already they knew his name, by means of an identification card found upon him, as well as a small packet of letters carefully pinned in an inner pocket of his coat. These last were all addressed in the same handwriting, which was undoubtedly feminine, to Andrew Denton. The card stated that

Andrew Denton, private, was formerly an insurance agent at Antwerp.

Doctor Gys had rather impatiently awaited the young man's return to consciousness that he might complete his examination. He now devoted the next half hour to a careful diagnosis of Denton's injuries. By this time the patient was suffering intense pain and a hypodermic injection of morphine was required to relieve him. When at last he was quietly drowsing the doctor called Maud aside to give her instructions.

"Watch him carefully," said he, "and don't let him suffer. Keep up the morphine."

"There is no hope, then?" she asked.

"Not the slightest. He may linger for days—even weeks, if we sustain his strength—but recovery is impossible. That bit of shell tore a horrible hole in the poor fellow and all we can do is keep him comfortable until the end. Without the morphine he would not live twelve hours."

"Shall I let him talk?"

"If he wishes to. His lungs are not involved, so it can do him no harm."

But Andrew Denton did not care to talk any more that day. He wanted to think, and lay quietly until Beth came on duty. To her he gave a smile and a word of thanks and again lapsed into thoughtful silence.

When Ajo brought the new consignment of wounded to the ship the doctors and nurses found themselves pretty busy for a time. With wounds to dress and one or two slight operations to perform, the afternoon passed swiftly away. The old patients must not be neglected, either, so Captain Carg said he would sit with the German and look after him, as he was able to converse with the patient in his own tongue.

The German was resting easily to-day but proved as glum and uncommunicative as ever. That did not worry the captain, who gave the man a cigarette and, when it was nonchalantly accepted, lighted his own pipe. Together they sat in silence and smoked, the German occupying an easy chair and resting his leg upon a stool, for he had refused to lie in a berth. Through the open window the dull boom of artillery could constantly be heard. After an hour or so:

"A long fight," remarked the captain in German.

The other merely looked at him, contemplatively. Carg stared for five minutes at the bandaged foot. Finally:

"Hard luck," said he.

This time the German nodded, looking at the foot also.

"In America," resumed the captain, puffing slowly, "they make fine artificial feet. Walk all right. Look natural."

"Vienna," said the German.

"Yes, I suppose so." Another pause.

"Name?" asked the German, with startling abruptness. But the other never winked.

"Carg. I'm a sailor. Captain of this ship. Live in Sangoa, when ashore."

"Sangoa?"

"Island in South Seas."

The wounded man reached for another cigarette and lighted it.

"Carg," he repeated, musingly. "German?"

"Why, my folks were, I believe. I've relations in Germany, yet. Munich. Visited them once, when a boy. Mother's name was Elbl. The Cargs lived next door to the Elbls. But they've lost track of me, and I of them. Nothing in common, you see."

The German finished his cigarette, looking at the captain at times reflectively. Carg, feeling his biography had not been appreciated, had lapsed into silence. At length the wounded man began feeling in his breast pocket—an awkward operation because the least action disturbed the swathed limb—and presently drew out a leather card case. With much deliberation he abstracted a card and handed it to the captain, who put on his spectacles and read:

"Otto Elbl. 12th Uhlans"

"Oh," he said, looking up to examine the German anew. "Otto Elbl of Munich?"

"Yes."

"H-m. Number 121 Friedrichstrasse?"

"Yes."

"I didn't see you when I visited your family. They said you were at college. Your father was William Elbl, my mother's brother."

The German stretched out his hand and gripped the fist of the captain.

"Cousins," he said.

Carg nodded, meditating.

"To be sure," he presently returned; "cousins. Have another cigarette."

CHAPTER XI

PATSY IS DEFIANT

That evening the captain joined Dr. Gys on deck.

"That German, Lieutenant Elbl," he began.

"Oh, is that his name?" asked Gys.

"Yes. Will he get well?"

"Certainly. What is a foot, to a man like him? But his soldiering days are past."

"Perhaps that's fortunate," returned the captain, ruminatively. "When I was a boy, his father was burgomaster—mayor—in Munich. People said he was well-to-do. The Germans are thrifty, so I suppose there's still money in the Elbl family."

"Money will do much to help reconcile the man to the loss of his foot," declared the doctor.

"Will he suffer much pain, while it is getting well?"

"Not if I can help it. The fellow bears pain with wonderful fortitude. When I was in Yucatan, and had to slash my face to get out the poisoned darts of the cactus, I screamed till you could have heard me a mile. And I had no anaesthetic to soothe me. Your lieutenant never whimpered or cringed with his mangled foot and he refused morphine when I operated on it. But I fooled him. I hate to see a brave man suffer. I stuck a needle just above the wound when he wasn't looking, and I've doped his medicine ever since."

"Thank you," said Carg; "he's my cousin."

In the small hours of the next morning, while Patsy was on duty in the hospital section, the young Belgian became wakeful and restless. She promptly administered a sedative and sat by his bedside. After a little his pain was eased and he became quiet, but he lay there with wide open eyes.

"Can I do anything more for you?" she asked.

"If you would be so kind," replied Andrew Denton.

"Well?"

"Please read to me some letters you will find in my pocket. I cannot read them myself, and—they will comfort me."

Patsy found the packet of letters.

"The top one first," he said eagerly. "Read them all!"

She opened the letter reluctantly. It was addressed in a dainty, female hand and the girl had the uncomfortable feeling that she was about to pry into personal relations of a delicate character.

"Your sweetheart?" she asked gently.

"Yes, indeed; my sweetheart and my wife."

"Oh, I see. And have you been married long?" He seemed a mere boy.

"Five months, but for the last two I have not seen her."

The letters were dated at Charleroi and each one began: "My darling husband." Patsy read the packet through, from first to last, her eyes filling with tears at times as she noted the rare devotion and passionate longing of the poor young wife and realized that the boyish husband was even now dying, a martyr to his country's cause. The letters were signed "Elizabeth." In one was a small photograph of a sweet, dark-eyed girl whom she instantly knew to be the bereaved wife.

"And does she still live at Charleroi?" Patsy asked.

"I hope so, mademoiselle; with her mother. The Germans now occupy the town, but you will notice the last letter states that all citizens are treated courteously and with much consideration, so I do not fear for her."

The reading of the letters, in conjunction with the opiate, seemed to comfort him, for presently he fell asleep. With a heavy heart the girl left him to attend to her other patients and at three o'clock Ajo came in and joined her, to relieve the tedium of the next three hours. The boy knew nothing of nursing, but he could help Patsy administer potions and change compresses and his presence was a distinct relief to her.

The girl was supposed to sleep from six o'clock—at which time she was relieved from duty—until one in the afternoon, but the next morning at eight she walked into the forward salon, where her friends were at breakfast, and sat down beside Uncle John.

"I could not sleep," said she, "because I am so worried over Andrew Denton."

"That is foolish, my dear," answered Mr. Merrick, affectionately patting the hand she laid in his. "The doctor says poor Denton cannot recover. If you're going to take to heart all the sad incidents we encounter on this hospital ship, it will not only ruin your usefulness but destroy your happiness."

"Exactly so," agreed Gys, coming into the salon in time to overhear this remark. "A nurse should be sympathetic, but impersonally so."

"Denton has been married but five months," said Patsy. "I have seen his wife's picture—she's a dear little girl!—and her letters to him are full of love and longing. She doesn't know, of course, of his—his accident—or that he—he—" Her voice broke with a sob she could not repress.

"M-m," purred Uncle John; "where does she live, this young wife?"

"At Charleroi."

"Well; the Germans are there."

"Yes, Uncle. But don't you suppose they would let her come to see her dying husband?"

"A young girl, unprotected? Would it be—safe?"

"The Germans," remarked Captain Carg from his end of the table, "are very decent people."

"Ahem!" said Uncle John.

"Some of them, I've no doubt, are quite respectable," observed Ajo; "but from all reports the rank and file, in war time, are—rather unpleasant to meet."

"Precisely," agreed Uncle John. "I think, Patsy dear, it will be best to leave this Belgian girl in ignorance of her husband's fate."

"I, myself, have a wife," quoth little Maurie, with smug assurance, "but she is not worrying about me, wherever she may be; nor do I feel especial anxiety for Clarette. A woman takes what comes—especially if she is obliged to."

Patsy regarded him indignantly.

"There are many kinds of women," she began.

"Thank heaven!" exclaimed Maurie, and then she realized how futile it was to argue with him.

A little later she walked on deck with Uncle John and pleaded her cause earnestly. It was said by those who knew him well that the kindly little gentleman was never able to refuse Patsy anything for long, and he was himself so well aware of this weakness that he made a supreme effort to resist her on this occasion.

"You and I," said she, "would have no trouble in passing the German lines. We are strictly neutral, you know, we Americans, and our passports and the Red Cross will take us anywhere in safety."

"It won't do, my dear," he replied. "You've already been in danger enough for one war. I shudder even now as I think of those bullets and shells at Nieuport."

"But we can pass through at some place where they are not fighting."

"Show me such a place!"

"And distances are very small in this part of the Continent. We could get to Charleroi in a day, and return the next day with Mrs. Denton."

"Impossible."

"The doctor says he may live for several days, but it may be only for hours. If you could see his face light up when he speaks of her, you would realize what a comfort her presence would be to him."

"I understand that, Patsy. But can't you see, my dear, that we're not able to do everything for those poor wounded soldiers? You have twenty in your charge now, and by to-night there may be possibly a dozen more. Many of them have wives at home, but—"

"But all are not dying, Uncle—and after only five months of married life, three of which they passed together. Here, at least, is one brave heart we may comfort, one poor woman who will be ever grateful for our generous kindness."

Mr. Merrick coughed. He wiped his eyes and blew his nose on his pink bordered handkerchief. But he made no promise.

Patsy left him and went to Ajo.

"See here," she said; "I'm going to Charleroi in an hour."

"It's a day's journey, Patsy."

"I mean I'm going to start in an hour. Will you go with me?"

"What does Uncle John say?" he inquired cautiously.

"I don't care what he says. I'm going!" she persisted, her eyes blazing with determination.

The boy whistled softly, studying her face. Then he walked across the deck to Mr. Merrick.

"Patsy is rampant, sir," said he. "She won't be denied. Go and argue with her, please."

"I *have* argued," returned Uncle John weakly.

"Well, argue again."

The little man cast a half frightened, half reproachful glance at his niece.

"Let's go and consult the doctor," he exclaimed, and together Uncle John and Ajo went below.

To their surprise, Gys supported Patsy's plea.

"He's a fine fellow, this Denton," said he, "and rather above the average soldier. Moreover, his case is a pitiful one. I'll agree to keep him alive until his wife comes."

Uncle John looked appealingly at Ajo.

"How on earth can we manage to cross the lines?" he asked.

"Take one of our launches," said the boy.

"Skim the coast to Ostend, and you'll avoid danger altogether."

"That's the idea!" exclaimed the doctor approvingly. "Why, it's the easiest thing in the world, sir."

Uncle John began to feel slightly reassured.

"Who will run the launch?" he inquired.

"I'll give you the captain and one of the men," said the boy. "Carg's an old traveler and knows more than he appears to. Besides, he speaks German. We can't spare very many, you understand, and the ambulances will keep Maurie and me pretty busy. Patsy will be missed, too, from the hospital ward, so you must hurry back."

"Two days ought to accomplish our object," said Uncle John.

"Easily," agreed Gys. "I've arranged for a couple of girls from the town to come and help us to-day, for I must save the strength of my expert nurses as much as possible, and I'll keep them with us until you return. The French girls are not experienced in nursing, but I'll take Miss Patsy's watch myself, so we shall get along all right."

Mr. Merrick and Jones returned to the deck.

"Well?" demanded Patsy.

"Get ready," said Uncle John; "we leave in an hour."

"For Charleroi?"

"Of course; unless you've changed your mind."

Patsy flew to her stateroom.

CHAPTER XII

THE OTHER SIDE

The launch in which they embarked bore the Red Cross on its sides, and an American flag floated from the bow and a Red Cross flag from the stern. Its four occupants wore the Red Cross uniforms. Yet three miles out of Dunkirk a shot came singing across their prow and they were obliged to lay to until a British man-of-war could lower a boat to investigate their errand. The coast is very shallow in this section, which permits boats of only the lightest draught to navigate in-shore, but the launch was able to skim over the surface at twelve miles an hour.

"This is pleasant!" grumbled Uncle John, as they awaited the approach of the warship's boat. "Our very appearance ought to insure us safe conduct, but I suppose that in these times every craft is regarded with suspicion."

The boat came alongside.

"Where are you going?" demanded an officer, gruffly.

"To Ostend."

"On what business?"

"Our own," replied Mr. Merrick.

"Be respectful, sir, or I'll arrest your entire outfit," warned the officer.

"You'll do nothing of the sort," declared Mr. Merrick. "You'll examine our papers, apologize for your interference and row back to your ship. We have the authority of the Red Cross to go wherever our duty calls us, and moreover we're American citizens. Permit me to add that we're in a hurry."

The officer turned first white and then red, but he appreciated the force of the argument.

"Your papers!" he commanded.

Uncle John produced them and waited patiently for their inspection, which was very deliberate. Finally the officer returned them and gave the order to his men to row back to the ship.

"One moment!" called Uncle John. "You haven't made the apology."

There was no answer. The boat moved swiftly away and at a gesture from Captain Carg the sailor started the launch again.

"I wonder why it is," mused Mr. Merrick, "that there is always this raspy feeling when the English meet Americans. On the surface we're friendly enough and our governments always express in diplomatic relations the most cordial good will; but I've always noticed in the English individual an undercurrent of antipathy for Americans that cannot be disguised. As a race the English hate us, I'm positive, and I wonder why?"

"I believe you're wrong, Uncle," remarked Patsy. "A few of the British may individually dislike us, but I'm sure the two nations are not antagonistic. Why should they be?"

"Yorktown," muttered the captain.

"I don't believe it," declared the girl. "They're too good sportsmen to bear grudges."

"All the same," persisted Uncle John, "the English have never favored us as the French have, or even the Russians."

From Dunkirk to Ostend, by the coast line, is only some twenty-five miles, yet although they started at a little after eleven o'clock it was three in the afternoon before they finally landed at the Belgian seaport. Interruptions were numerous, and although they were treated courteously, in the main, it was only after rigid questioning and a thorough examination that they were permitted to proceed. A full hour was consumed at the harbor at Ostend before they could even land.

As they stepped upon the wharf a group of German soldiers met them and now Captain Carg became the spokesman of the party.

The young officer in command removed his helmet to bow deferentially to Patsy and then turned to ask their business at Ostend.

"He says we must go before the military governor," said Carg, translating. "There, if our papers are regular, permits will be issued for us to proceed to Charleroi."

They left the sailor in charge of the launch, which was well provisioned and contained a convertible bunk, and followed the officer into the town. Ostend is a large city, fortified, and was formerly one of the most important ports on the North Sea, as well as a summer resort of prominence. The city now being occupied by the Germans, our friends found few citizens on the streets of Ostend and these hurried nervously on their way. The streets swarmed with German soldiery.

Arriving at headquarters they found that the commandant was too busy to attend to the Red Cross Americans. He ordered them taken before Colonel Grau for examination.

"But why examine us at all?" protested Mr. Merrick. "Doesn't our sacred mission protect us from such annoying details?"

The young officer regretted that it did not. They would find Colonel Grau in one of the upper rooms. It would be a formal examination, of course, and brief. But busy spies had even assumed the insignia of the Red Cross to mask their nefarious work and an examination was therefore necessary as a protective measure. So they ascended a broad staircase and proceeded along a corridor to the colonel's office.

Grau was at the head of the detective service at Ostend and invested with the task of ferreting out the numerous spies in the service of the Allies and dealing with them in a summary manner. He was a very stout man, and not very tall. His eyes were light blue and his grizzled mustache was a poor imitation of that affected by the Kaiser. When Grau looked up, on their entrance, Patsy decided that their appearance had startled him, but presently she realized that the odd expression was permanent.

In a chair beside the colonel's desk sat, or rather lounged, another officer, encased in a uniform so brilliant that it arrested the eye before one could discover its contents. These were a wizened, weather-beaten man of advanced age, yet rugged as hickory. His eyes had a periodical squint; his brows wore a persistent frown. There was a broad scar on his left cheek and another across his forehead. A warrior who had seen service, probably, but whose surly physiognomy was somewhat disconcerting.

The two officers had been in earnest conversation, but when Mr. Merrick's party was ushered in, the elder man leaned back in his chair, squinting and scowling, and regarded them silently.

"Huh!" exclaimed the colonel, in a brusque growl. "What is it, von Holtz?"

The young officer explained that the party had just arrived from Dunkirk in a launch; the commandant had asked Colonel Grau kindly to examine them. Uncle John proceeded to state the case, Captain Carg interpreting. They operated a Red Cross hospital ship at Dunkirk, and one of their patients, a young Belgian, was dying of his wounds. They had come to find his young wife and take her back with them to Dunkirk in their launch, that she might comfort the last moments of her husband. The Americans asked for safe conduct to Charleroi, and permission to take Mrs. Denton with them to Dunkirk. Then he presented his papers, including the authority of the American Red Cross Society, the letter from the secretary of state and the recommendation of the German ambassador at Washington.

The colonel looked them all over. He uttered little guttural exclamations and tapped the desk with his finger-tips as he read, and all the time his face wore that perplexing expression of surprise. Finally he asked:

"Which is Mr. Merrick?"

Hearing his name, Uncle John bowed.

"Huh! But the description does not fit you."

Captain Carg translated this.

"Why not?" demanded Uncle John.

"It says you are short, stout, blue-eyed, bald, forty-five years of age."

"Of course."

"You are not short; I think you are as tall as I am. Your eyes are not blue; they are olive green. You are not bald, for there is still hair over your ears. Huh! How do you explain that?"

"It's nonsense," said Uncle John scornfully.

Carg was more cautious in interpreting the remark. He assured the colonel, in German, that the description of Mr. Merrick was considered close enough for all practical purposes. But Grau was not satisfied. He went over the papers again and then turned to face the other officer.

"What do you think, General?" he asked, hesitatingly.

"Suspicious!" was the reply.

"I think so, myself," said the colonel. "Mark you: Here's a man who claims to come from Sangoa, a place no one has ever heard of; and the other has endorsements purporting to come from the highest officials in America. Huh! what does it mean?"

"Papers may be forged, or stolen from their proper owners," suggested the squinting general. "This excuse of coming here to get the wife of a hurt Belgian seems absurd. If they are really Red Cross workers, they are not attending to their proper business."

When the captain interpreted this speech Patsy said angrily:

"The general is an old fool."

"An idiot, I'll call him," added Uncle John. "I wish I could tell him so."

"You *have* told him," said the general in good English, squinting now more rapidly than ever, "and your manner of speech proves you to be impostors. I have never known a respectable Red Cross nurse, of any country, who called a distinguished officer a fool—and to his face."

"I didn't know you understood English," she said.

"That is no excuse!"

"But I *did* know," she added, "that I had judged you correctly. No one with a spark of intelligence could doubt the evidence of these papers."

"The papers are all right. Where did you get them?"

"From the proper authorities."

He turned to speak rapidly in German to Colonel Grau, who had been uneasy during the conversation in English, because he failed to understand it. His expression of piquant surprise was intensified as he now turned to the Americans.

"You may as well confess your imposture," said he. "It will make your punishment lighter. However, if on further examination you prove to be spies, your fate is beyond my power to mitigate."

"See here," said Uncle John, when this was translated to him, "if you dare to interfere with us, or cause us annoyance, I shall insist on your being courtmartialed. You are responsible to your superiors, I suppose, and they dare not tolerate an insult to the Red Cross, nor to an American citizen. You may have the sense to consider that if these papers and letters are genuine, as I declare they are, I have friends powerful enough to bring this matter before the Kaiser himself, in which case someone will suffer a penalty, even if he is a general or a colonel."

As he spoke he glared defiantly at the older officer, who calmly proceeded to translate the speech to the colonel. Carg reported that it was translated verbatim. Then the general sat back and squinted at his companion, who seemed fairly bewildered by the threat. Patsy caught the young officer smothering a smile, but neither of them interrupted the silence that followed.

Once again the colonel picked up the papers and gave them a rigid examination, especially that of the German ambassador, which was written in his own language. "I cannot understand," he muttered, "how one insignificant American citizen could secure such powerful endorsements. It has never happened before in my experience."

"It is extraordinary," said the general.

"Mr. Merrick," said Patsy to him, "is a very important man in America. He is so important that any indignity to him will be promptly resented."

"I will investigate your case further," decided Colonel Grau, after another sotto voce conference with the general. "Spies are getting to be very clever, these days, and we cannot take chances. However, I assure you there is no disposition to worry you and until your standing is determined you will be treated with every consideration."

"Do you mean that we are prisoners?" asked Uncle John, trying to control his indignation.

"No, indeed. You will be detained, of course, but you are not prisoners—as yet. I will keep your papers and submit them to the general staff. It will be for that august body to decide."

Uncle John protested vigorously; Patsy faced the old general and told him this action was an outrage that would be condemned by the entire civilized world; Captain Carg gravely assured both officers that they were making a serious mistake. But nothing could move the stolid Germans. The general, indeed, smiled grimly and told them in English that he was in no way responsible, whatever happened. This was Colonel Grau's affair, but he believed, nevertheless, that the colonel was acting wisely.

The young officer, who had stood like a statue during the entire interview, was ordered to accompany the Americans to a hotel, where they must be kept under surveillance but might follow, to an extent, their own devices. They were not to mail letters nor send telegrams.

The officer asked who should guard the suspects.

"Why not yourself, Lieutenant? You are on detached duty, I believe?"

"At the port, Colonel."

"There are too many officers at the port; it is a sinecure. I will appoint you to guard the Americans. You speak their language, I believe?"

The young man bowed.

"Very well; I shall hold you responsible for their safety."

They were then dismissed and compelled to follow their guard from the room.

Patsy was now wild with rage and Uncle John speechless. Even Carg was evidently uneasy.

"Do not mind," said the young lieutenant consolingly. "It is merely a temporary inconvenience, you know, for your release will come very soon. And since you are placed in my care I beg you to accept this delay with good grace and be happy as possible. Ostend is full of life and I am conducting you to an excellent hotel."

CHAPTER XIII

TARDY JUSTICE

The courtesy of Lieutenant von Holtz was beyond criticism. He obtained for his charges a comfortable suite of rooms in an overcrowded hotel, obliging the landlord to turn away other guests that Mr. Merrick's party might be accommodated. The dinner that was served in their cosy sitting room proved excellent, having been ordered by von Holtz after he had requested that privilege. When the young officer appeared to see that it was properly served, Patsy invited him to join them at the table and he laughingly consented.

"You are one of our party, by force of circumstances," said the girl, "and since we've found you good-natured and polite, and believe you are not to blame for our troubles, we may as well be friendly while we are together."

The young man was evidently well pleased.

"However evil your fortune may be," said he, "I cannot fail to be impressed by my own good luck. Perhaps you may guess what a relief this pleasant commission is to one who for days has been compelled to patrol those vile smelling docks, watching for spies and enduring all sorts of weather."

"To think," said Uncle John gloomily, "that *we* are accused of being spies!"

"It is not for me," returned von Holtz, "to criticize the acts of my superiors. I may say, however, that were it my province to decide the question, you would now be free. Colonel Grau has an excellent record for efficiency and seldom makes a mistake, but I suspect his judgment was influenced by the general, whose son was once jilted by an American girl."

"We're going to get even with them both, before this affair is ended," declared Patsy, vindictively; "but although you are our actual jailer I promise that you will escape our vengeance."

"My instructions are quite elastic, as you heard," said the lieutenant. "I am merely ordered to keep you in Ostend, under my eye, until your case has been passed upon by the commandant or the general staff. Since you have money, you may enjoy every luxury save that of travel, and I ask you to command my services in all ways consistent with my duty."

"What worries me," said Patsy to Uncle John, "is the delay. If we are kept here for long, poor Denton will die before we can find his wife and take her to him."

"How long are we liable to be detained?" Uncle John asked the officer.

"I cannot say. Perhaps the council of the general staff will meet to-morrow morning; perhaps not for several days," was the indefinite reply.

Patsy wiped away the tears that began to well into her eyes. She had so fondly set her heart on reuniting the Dentons that her disappointment was very great.

Von Holtz noticed the girl's mood and became thoughtful. Captain Carg had remained glum and solemn ever since they had left the colonel's office. Uncle John sat in silent indignation, wondering what could be done to influence these stupid Germans. Presently the lieutenant remarked:

"That sailor whom you left with the launch seemed an intelligent fellow."

Patsy gave a start; Uncle John looked at the young man expectantly; the captain nodded his head as he slowly replied:

"Henderson is one of the picked men I brought from Sangoa. He is both intelligent and loyal."

"Curiously enough," said von Holtz, "I neglected to place the man under arrest. I even forgot to report him. He is free."

"Ah!" exclaimed Patsy, her eyes lighting.

"I know a civilian here—a bright young Belgian—who is my friend and will do anything I ask of him," resumed von Holtz, still musingly. "I had the good fortune to protect his mother when our troops entered the city, and he is grateful."

Patsy was thinking very fast now.

"Could Henderson get to Charleroi, do you imagine?" she asked. "He has a passport."

"We do not consider passports of much value," said the officer; "but a Red Cross appointment—"

"Oh, he has that, too; all our men carry them."

"In that case, with my friend Rondel to guide him, I believe Henderson could accomplish your errand."

"Let us send for him at once!" exclaimed Uncle John.

Carg scribbled on a card.

"He wouldn't leave the launch without orders, unless forced by the Germans," asserted the captain, and handed the card to von Holtz.

The young lieutenant took his cap, bowed profoundly and left the room. In ten minutes he returned, saying: "I am not so fortunate as I had thought. All our troops are on the move, headed for the Yser. There will be fighting, presently, and—I must remain here," he added despondently.

"It won't be your last chance, I'm sure," said Patsy. "Will that dreadful Colonel Grau go, too?"

"No; he is to remain. But all regiments quartered here are now marching out and to-morrow a fresh brigade will enter Ostend."

They were silent a time, until someone rapped upon the door. Von Holtz admitted a slim, good-looking young Belgian who grasped his hand and said eagerly in French:

"You sent for me?"

"Yes. You may speak English here, Monsieur Rondel." Then he presented his friend to the Americans, who approved him on sight.

Henderson came a few minutes later and listened respectfully to the plan Miss Doyle unfolded. He was to go with Monsieur Rondel to Charleroi, find Mrs. Denton, explain that her husband was very ill, and bring her back with him to Ostend. He would report promptly on his return and they would tell him what to do next.

The man accepted the mission without a word of protest. Charleroi was in central Belgium, but that did not mean many miles away and Rondel assured him they would meet with no difficulties. The trains were reserved for soldiers, but the Belgian had an automobile and a German permit to drive it. The roads were excellent.

"Now, remember," said Patsy, "the lady you are going for is Mrs. Albert Denton. She lives with her mother, or did, the last we heard of her."

"And her mother's name and address?" inquired Henderson.

"We are ignorant of either," she confessed; "but it's not a very big town and I'm sure you'll easily find her."

"I know the place well," said Rondel, "and I have friends residing there who will give me information."

Uncle John supplied them liberally with money, impressed upon them the necessity of haste, and sent them away. Rondel declared the night time was best for the trip and promised to be on the way within the hour, and in Charleroi by next morning.

Notwithstanding the fact that they had succeeded in promoting by proxy the mission which had brought them to Belgium, the Americans found the next day an exceedingly irksome one. In the company of Lieutenant von Holtz they were permitted to walk about the city, but they found little pleasure in that, owing to the bustle of outgoing troops and the arrival of others to replace them. Nor did they care to stray far from their quarters, for fear the council would meet and they might be sent for.

However, no sign from Colonel Grau was received that day. Patsy went to bed with a nervous headache and left Uncle John and the captain to smoke more than was good for them. Both the men had now come to regard their situation as serious and as the American consul was at this time absent in Brussels they could think of no way to secure their freedom. No one knew when the consul would return; Mr. Merrick had been refused the privilege of using the telegraph or mails. During one of their strolls they had met the correspondent of an American newspaper, but when the man learned they were suspects he got away from them as soon as possible. He did not know Mr. Merrick and his own liberty was too precarious for him to argue with Colonel Grau.

"I'm beginning to think," said Uncle John, "that we're up against a hard proposition. Letters and endorsements from prominent Americans seem to have no weight with these Germans. I'd no idea our identity could ever be disputed."

"We must admit, sir," returned the captain, reflectively, "that the spy system in this war is something remarkable. Spies are everywhere; clever ones, too, who adopt every sort of subterfuge to escape detection. I do not blame Grau so much for caution as for lack of judgment."

"He's a blockhead!" cried Mr. Merrick testily.

"He is. I'm astonished they should place so much power in the hands of one so slow witted."

"He has insulted us," continued Uncle John. "He has dared to arrest three free-born Americans."

"Who came into a troubled country, occupied by a conquering army, without being invited."

"Well—that's true," sighed the little millionaire, "but what are we going to do about it?"

"Wait," counseled the captain.

The next day dawned dark and rainy and the weather had a depressing effect upon the prisoners. It was too damp to stir out of doors and the confinement of the hotel rooms became especially irksome. Not only were they anxious about their own fate but it was far past the time when they should have heard from Henderson and Rondel. Patsy's nerves were getting beyond her control; Uncle John stumped around with his hands thrust deep in his pockets and a frown wrinkling his forehead; the captain smoked innumerable pipes of tobacco and said not a word. Von Holtz, noting the uneasiness of his charges, discreetly forbore conversation and retired to a far corner where he hid behind a book.

It was nearing evening when a commotion was heard on the stairs, followed by the heavy tramp of feet in the corridor. A sharp rap sounded on the door of their sitting room. Uncle John stepped forward to open it, when in stalked a group of German officers, their swords and spurs clanking and their cloaks glistening with rain-drops. At sight of the young girl off came cap and helmet and with one accord they bowed low.

The leader was a tall, thin man with a leathern face, hooked nose and piercing gray eyes. His breast glittered with orders. It was von Kargenbrut, the military governor.

"Pardon our intrusion," he said in English, his harsh voice having a guttural accent. "Which gentleman is Mr. John Merrick?"

"I am John Merrick."

The eagle eyes swept over him with a swift glance.

"We owe you our apology," continued the governor, speaking as fiercely as if he were ordering Uncle John beheaded. "I have been too busy to take up your case before to-day, when I discover that we have treated you discourteously. You will consider our fault due to these troubled times, when mistakes occur in spite of our watchfulness. Is it not so?"

"Your error has caused us great inconvenience," responded Mr. Merrick stiffly.

The governor whirled around. "Colonel Grau!" he called, and from the rear of the group the colonel stepped forward. His face still wore the expression of comical surprise. "Return to Mr. Merrick his papers and credentials."

The colonel drew the packet of papers from his breast pocket and handed it to Uncle John. Then he glanced hesitatingly at his superior, who glared at him.

"He cannot speak the English," said the governor to Mr. Merrick, "but he owes you reparation."

"Grau's stupidity has been very annoying, to say the least," was the ungracious reply. "We came here on important business, and presented our papers—all in proper order—on demand. We had the right to expect decent treatment, as respectable American citizens engaged in humanitarian work; yet this—this—man," pointing an accusing finger at the colonel, "ordered us detained—arrested!—and kept our papers."

The governor listened coldly and at the end of the speech inclined his head.

"Colonel Grau," said he, "has been relieved of his duties here and transferred to another station. To you I have personally apologized. You will find my endorsement on your papers and, in addition, an order that will grant you safe conduct wherever you may wish to go. If that is not enough, make your demands and I will consider them."

"Why, that is all I can expect, your Excellency, under the circumstances," replied Mr. Merrick. "I suppose I ought to thank you for your present act of justice."

"No; it is your due. Good evening, Mr. Merrick."

He swung around on his heel and every officer of the group turned with him, like so many automatons, all facing the door. But Mr. Merrick touched the governor upon the arm.

"One moment, your Excellency. This young officer, Lieutenant von Holtz, has treated us kindly and courteously. I want you to know that one of your men, at least, has performed his duty in a way to merit our thanks—and yours."

The governor scowled at Lieutenant von Holtz, who stood like a statue, with lowered eyes.

"Lieutenant, you are commissioned to guide Mr. Merrick as long as he remains within our lines. You will guard his safety and that of his party. When he departs, come to me personally with your report."

The young officer bowed; the governor tramped to the door and went out, followed by his staff. Grau left the room last, with hang-dog look, and Patsy slammed the door in the hope of bumping his wooden head.

"So we're free?" she said, turning to von Holtz.

"Not only that, Fraulein, but you are highly favored," he replied. "All German territory is now open to you."

"It's about time they came to their senses," remarked Uncle John, with a return to his accustomed cheerfulness.

"And, best of all," said Patsy exultantly, "they've fired that awful colonel!"

The captain thoughtfully filled and lighted his pipe.

"I wonder," said he, "how that happened. Was it the council, do you think, Lieutenant?"

Von Holtz shook his head.

"I think it was the governor," he replied. "He is a just man, and had you been able to see him personally on your arrival you would have been spared any annoyance."

"Perhaps," said Patsy doubtfully. "But your governor's a regular bear."

"I believe that is merely his way," asserted Uncle John. "I didn't mind the man's tone when I found his words and deeds were all right. But he—"

Another rap at the door. Patsy opened it and admitted Henderson. He saluted the captain, bowed to the others and said:

"We've got her, sir."

"Mrs. Denton?" cried Patsy, delightedly.

Henderson nodded.

"Yes, Miss Doyle; Mrs. Denton and the children."

"The children! Why, there aren't any."

"I beg your pardon, Miss; there are two."

"Two children!" she exclaimed in dismay. "There must be some mistake. The young people have only been married five months."

Henderson stood stiff as a poker, refusing to argue the point.

"A governess, maybe," suggested the captain.

"More likely," said Uncle John, "young Denton married a widow, with—eh—eh—incumbrances."

"That's it, sir," said Henderson earnestly.

"What's it?"

"The incumbrances, sir. No other word could describe 'em."

Patsy's heart sank; she was greatly disappointed.

"And she so young and pretty!" she murmured.

Henderson started to smile, but quickly suppressed it.

"Shall I show them up, Miss?" he inquired.

"Of course," answered Uncle John, as the girl hesitated. "You should have brought her to us at once. Where is that Belgian—Rondel?"

"He is guarding the woman, sir."

"Guarding her!"

"She's a little difficult to manage, sir, at times. She left Charleroi willingly enough, but she's tricky, and it is our duty to deliver her to you safely."

"Get her at once, Henderson," exclaimed Patsy, recovering her wits; "and the dear children, too."

Presently there was a sound of shuffling on the stairs and through the corridor. The door opened to admit the arrivals from Charleroi.

Henderson first pushed in a big woman dressed in a faded blue-checked gown, belted around the waist in a manner that made her look like a sack tied in the middle. Her head was bare, her hair awry, her face sullen and hard; she was undeniably "fleshy" and not altogether clean. She resisted Henderson at every step and glared around her with shrewd and shifting eyes.

Following her came Monsieur Rondel leading a boy and a girl, the latter being a small replica of the woman. The boy was viciously struggling to bite the hand of the Belgian, who held him fast.

"Ah, well," said Rondel, first sighing and then turning with a smile to face the lieutenant, "we have performed our mission. But heaven guard us from another like it!"

Patsy stared hard at the woman.

"This cannot be Mrs. Denton," she gasped, bewildered.

"Indeed?" answered Rondel in English. "She declares that is her name. Question her in French or Flemish, Miss Doyle."

Patsy addressed the woman in French but could elicit no reply. She stood impassive and silent.

"How did you make the mistake?" asked the girl, looking reproachfully first at Henderson and then at Rondel, both of whom were evidently astonished to find themselves at fault. "I have seen a photograph of Mrs. Andrew Denton, taken recently, and she is young and pretty and—and—rather small."

Monsieur Rondel cleared his throat to answer:

"It happened in this way, mademoiselle: We searched one whole day in Charleroi for Mrs. Denton but could not find her. My friends, on whom I had relied for assistance, had unfortunately moved away or joined the army. The townspeople were suspicious of Monsieur Henderson, who is a foreigner. We could get no information whatever. I appealed to the burgomaster and he said he would try to find Mrs. Denton for us the next day. In the morning came to us this woman, who said she was the person we sought. If we promised her safe conduct to Dunkirk, she would go with us. She had wanted to go to Dunkirk for some weeks, but the Germans would not let her pass the lines. We suspected nothing wrong, for she admitted she was aware that her husband is in Dunkirk, and she wanted to get to him. So we brought her to you."

Patsy faced the woman resolutely and said in French:

"Why did you wish to get to Dunkirk?"

"He has said it. To find my husband," replied the woman in a surly tone.

"What is your name?"

No reply.

"Answer me!"

The woman eyed her obstinately and remained silent.

"Very well. Release those children, Monsieur Rondel. Madam, you have imposed upon us; you have tricked us in order to get to Ostend at our expense. Now go, and take your children with you."

She pointed dramatically at the door, but the woman retained her position, only moving to cuff the boy, who was kicking Henderson on his shins. Then, setting her hands on her hips she said defiantly:

"They promised me passage to Dunkirk, and they must take me there."

"Who promised you?"

"Those men," pointing to them, "and the burgomaster."

"Yes," admitted Henderson, "we agreed with the burgomaster to take her out of the country. We signed a paper to that effect."

"But she is a Belgian. And she is not the person she claimed to be."

To this neither Rondel nor Henderson had an answer.

"See here," said Uncle John, "I'll untangle this matter in a jiffy. Here is money; give it to the woman and tell her to get out—or we'll eject her by force."

The woman grabbed the money eagerly, but after placing it in an ample pocket she said: "I will go no place but Dunkirk. I will not leave you until you take me there."

But here the lieutenant interfered. He suddenly faced the woman, who had not noticed his presence before, and she shrank back in fear at sight of his uniform. The boy and girl both began to cry.

"I know you," said von Holtz sternly. "You are the wife of a spy who has been condemned to death by both the Belgians and the Germans, since he betrayed them both. The last time you came to Ostend to annoy us you were driven out of the city. There is still an edict against you. Will you leave this room peaceably, or shall I order you under arrest?"

"Dog of a German!" she hissed, "the day is coming when I will help to drive you out of Belgium, even as you now drive me. Brave soldiers are you, to make war on women and children. Guh! I would kill you where you stand—if I dared." With venomous hate she spat upon the floor, then seized her wailing children, shook them and waddled out of the room.

There was a general sigh of relief.

"You may return to the launch, Henderson," said the captain.

"Monsieur Rondel," said Uncle John, grasping the young Belgian's hand, "we are grateful to you for your kindness. The failure of your mission was not your fault. We thank you. The governor has given us our liberty and permission to travel where we please, so to-morrow we will go to Charleroi ourselves to search for Mrs. Denton."

"My motor car is at your disposal, sir, and my services."

"To-morrow? Oh, let us go to-night, Uncle!" cried Patsy.

Mr. Merrick looked inquiringly at the Belgian.

"I am ready now," said Rondel with a bow.

"Then," said Patsy, "we will start in half an hour. You see, we have wasted two whole days—two precious days! I hope Dr. Gys will keep his promise, and that we shall find poor Denton alive on our return."

CHAPTER XIV

FOUND AT LAST

The pretty city of Charleroi had suffered little damage from the German invasion, yet many of the townspeople had gone away since the occupation and those who remained kept well within their houses or huddled in anxious groups upon the streets. The civic affairs were still administered by the Belgian burgomaster, but the martial law of the Germans prevailed over all.

When Patsy Doyle, escorted by Uncle John and accompanied by Captain Carg, Lieutenant von Holtz and Monsieur Rondel, arrived in the early morning, the streets were comparatively deserted. The Hotel Royal received them hospitably and the landlord and his daughters prepared them an excellent breakfast.

While eating, Patsy chatted with the Belgian girls, who were neat, modest and intelligent. She found that Henderson and Rondel had not stopped at this hotel while in Charleroi, but at a smaller inn at the other end of the town. The girls remembered hearing of their visit and of their inquiries for a Mrs. Denton, but did not know whether they had succeeded in their quest or not.

"We have lived here all our lives," said the eldest of the landlord's three daughters, "but we have not known, during that time, any family of Dentons in Charleroi."

Patsy reflected.

"They were married only five months ago, these Dentons," said she, "and the young man may have come from some other town. Do you remember that any of your young girls were married about five months ago?"

Yes; there was Hildegarde Bentel, but she had married Anthony Mattison, who was not a soldier. Could the American mamselle remember what the girl's first name was?

"Oh, yes!" exclaimed Patsy. "She signed her letters 'Elizabeth.'"

They shook their heads.

"My name is also Elizabeth," said one. "We have many Elizabeths in Charleroi, but none has lately married."

"And her husband told me that she was now living here with her mother."

"Ah, let us see, then," responded another. "Could she have been a lady of rank, think you?"

"I—I do not know."

"Is her husband an officer?"

"No; a private, I believe."

"Then we are on the wrong scent," laughed the girl. "I had in mind the daughter of the Countess Voig, whose name chances to be Elizabeth. She was educated at a convent in Antwerp, and the countess has lived in that city for several years, in order to be nearer her daughter. There was some gossip here that the young lady had married in Antwerp, just after leaving the convent; but we know little of the life of the Voigs because they are very reserved. Two or three months ago they returned to their castle, which is four miles to the north of Charleroi, and there they are still living in retirement. Every day the old steward drives into town to visit the post office, but we have not seen the countess nor her daughter since they came back."

Patsy related this news to Uncle John, who did not understand French.

"Let us drive over to Castle Voig the first thing," she said.

"But, my dear, it's unreasonable," he objected. "Do you suppose a high-born young lady would marry a common soldier? In America, where we have no caste, it would be quite probable, but here—"

"He wasn't a soldier five months ago," said Patsy. "He's just a volunteer, who joined the army when his country needed him, as many of the wealthy and aristocratic Belgians did. He may be high-born himself, for all we know. At any rate I mean to visit that castle. Tell Rondel to bring around the automobile."

They had no trouble in passing the guards, owing to the presence of von Holtz, and in half an hour they were rolling through a charming, peaceful country that as yet had suffered no blemish through the German conquest.

At Castle Voig they were received by an aged retainer who was visibly nervous at their arrival. He eyed the uniform of young von Holtz with ill-concealed terror and hurried away to carry their cards to the countess. After a long wait they learned that the countess would receive the Americans, but it was a full half hour after that when they were ushered into a reception room where a lady sat in solitary state.

Under other circumstances Patsy could have spent a day in admiring the quaint, old-fashioned furniture and pictures and the wonderful carvings of the beamed ceiling, but now she was so excited that she looked only at the countess. The lady was not very imposing in form or dress but her features were calm and dignified and she met her guests with a grave courtesy that was impressive if rather chilly. Before Patsy had summoned courage to explain her errand a younger woman—almost a girl—hurriedly entered the room and took a position beside the other.

"Oh, it's Elizabeth—it really is!" cried Patsy, clapping her hands together joyfully.

Mother and daughter regarded the American girl wonderingly and somewhat haughtily, but Patsy was not in the least dismayed.

"Isn't this Mrs. Denton?" she asked, stepping forward to lay a hand upon the other girl's arm.

"Yes," was the quiet reply.

Patsy's great eyes regarded her a moment with so sad and sympathetic a look that Mrs. Denton shrank away. Then she noticed for the first time the Red Cross uniform, and her hand went swiftly to her heart as she faltered:

"You—you have brought bad news of Andrew—of my husband?"

"Yes, I am sorry to admit that it is bad news," answered Patsy soberly. "He has been wounded and is now lying ill in our hospital ship at Dunkirk. We came here to find you, and to take you to him."

Mrs. Denton turned to her mother, a passionate appeal in her eyes. But it was some moments before the hard, set look on the face of the countess softened. It did soften at last, however, and she turned to Patsy and said simply:

"We will prepare for the journey at once. Pray excuse us; Niklas will serve refreshments. We will not detain you long."

As they turned to leave the room Elizabeth Denton suddenly seized Patsy's hand.

"He will live?" she whispered. "Tell me he will live!"

Patsy's heart sank, but she summoned her wits by an effort.

"I am not a surgeon, my dear, and do not know how serious the wound may be," she answered, "but I assure you it will gladden his heart to see you again. He thinks and speaks only of you."

The girl-wife studied her face a moment and then dropped her hand and hurried after her mother.

"I fibbed, Uncle," said Patsy despondently. "I fibbed willfully. But— how could I help it when she looked at me that way?"

CHAPTER XV

DR. GYS SURPRISES HIMSELF

Henderson was waiting with the launch at the Ostend docks. Lieutenant von Holtz was earnestly thanked by Patsy and Uncle John for his kindness and in return he exacted a promise from them to hunt him up in Germany some day, when the war was ended. The countess and Mrs. Denton, sad and black-robed, had been made comfortable in the stern seats of the boat and the captain was just about to order Henderson to start the engine when up to them rushed the fat Belgian woman and her two children.

Without an instant's hesitation the two youngsters leaped aboard like cats and their mother would have followed but for the restraining hand of Captain Carg.

"What does this mean?" cried Mr. Merrick angrily.

The woman jabbered volubly in French.

"She says," interpreted Patsy, "that we promised to take her to Dunkirk, so she may find her husband."

"Let her walk!" said Uncle John.

"The Germans won't allow her to cross the lines. What does it matter, Uncle? We have plenty of room. In three hours we can be rid of them, and doubtless the poor thing is really anxious to find her lost husband, who was last seen in Dunkirk."

"He is a spy, and a traitor to both sides, according to report."

"That isn't our affair, is it? And I suppose even people of that class have hearts and affections."

"Well, let her come aboard, Captain," decided Uncle John. "We can't waste time in arguing."

They stowed her away in the bow, under Henderson's care, and threatened the children with dire punishment if they moved from under her shadow. Then the launch sped out into the bay and away toward Dunkirk.

Three days had brought many changes to the hospital ship *Arabella*. Of the original batch of patients only Lieutenant Elbl, the German, and Andrew Denton now remained. All the others had been sent home, transferred to the government hospitals or gone back to the front, according to the character of their injuries. This was necessary because their places were needed by the newly wounded who were brought each day from the front. Little Maurie was driving the ambulance again and, with Ajo beside him and Dr. Kelsey and a sailor for assistants, the Belgian would make a dash to Ypres or Dixmude or Furnes and return with a full load of wounded soldiers.

These were the days of the severest fighting in Flanders, fighting so severe that it could not keep up for long. There would come a lull presently, when the overworked nurses and surgeons could get a bit of sleep and draw a long breath again.

Gys had elected to remain aboard the ship, where with Maud and Beth he was kept busy night and day. Two French girls—young women of good birth and intelligence—had been selected by Dr. Gys from a number of applicants as assistant nurses, and although they were inexperienced, their patriotic zeal rendered them valuable. They now wore the Red Cross uniforms and it was decided to retain them as long as the ship's hospital remained crowded.

There was plenty of work for all and the worry and long hours might have broken down the health and strength of Beth and Maud had not the doctor instituted regular periods of duty for each member of the force and insisted on the schedule being carried out.

This hospital ship was by no means so gloomy a place as the reader may imagine. The soldiers were prone to regard their hurts lightly, as "a bit of hard luck," and since many had slight injuries it was customary for them to gather in groups upon the deck, where they would laugh and chat together, play cards for amusement or smoke quantities of cigarettes. They were mainly kind-hearted and grateful fellows and openly rejoiced that the misfortunes of war had cast their lot on this floating hospital.

Under the probe of the surgeon to-day, a fortnight hence back on the firing line, was not very unusual with these brave men. The ambulances had gathered in a few German soldiers, who would become prisoners of war on their recovery, and while these were inclined to be despondent and unsociable they were treated courteously by all, the Americans showing no preference for any nation. The large majority of the patients, however, came from the ranks of the Allies—French, English and Belgian—and these were men who could smile and be merry with bandaged heads, arms a-sling, legs in splints, bullet holes here and there, such afflictions being regarded by their victims with a certain degree of pride.

Dr. Gys was in his element, for now he had ample opportunity to display his skill and his patients were unable to "jump to another doctor" in case his ugly features revolted them. His main interest, however, lay in the desperately wounded Belgian private, Andrew Denton, whom he had agreed to keep alive until the return of Miss Doyle and her uncle.

In making this promise Gys had figured on a possible delay of several days, but on the second day following Patsy's departure the sudden sinking of his patient aroused a defiant streak in the surgeon and he decided to adopt drastic measures in order to prevent Denton from passing away before his wife's arrival.

"I want you to assist me in a serious operation," he said to Maud Stanton. "By all the rules and precedents of human flesh, that fellow Denton ought to succumb to his wound within the next three hours. The shell played havoc with his interior and I have never dared, until now, to attempt to patch things up; but if we're going to keep him alive until morning, or until your cousin's return, we must accomplish the impossible."

"What is that?" she inquired.

"Remove his vital organs, tinker them up and put them back so they will work properly."

"Can that be done, doctor?"

"I think not. But I'm going to try it. I am positive that if we leave him alone he has less than three hours of life remaining; so, if we fail, Miss Stanton, as it is reasonable to expect, poor Denton will merely be spared a couple of hours of pain. Get the anaesthetics, please."

With all her training and experience as a nurse, Maud was half terrified at the ordeal before her. But she realized the logic of the doctor's conclusion and steeled her nerves to do her part.

An hour later she stood looking down upon the patient. He was still upon the operating table but breathing quietly and as strongly as at any time since he had received his wound.

"This shows," Dr. Gys said to her, his voice keen with elation, "what fools we are to take any human condition for granted. Man is a machine. Smash his mechanism and it cannot work; make the proper repairs before it is too late and—there he goes, ticking away as before. Not as good a machine as it was prior to the break, but with care and caution it will run a long time."

"He will live, then, you think?" she asked softly, marveling that after what she had witnessed the man was still able to breathe.

Gys leaned down and put his ear to the heart of the patient. For two minutes he remained motionless. Then he straightened up and a smile spread over his disfigured features.

"I confidently believe, Miss Stanton, we have turned the trick! Luck, let us call it, for no sensible surgeon would have attempted the thing. Rest assured that Andrew Denton will live for the next ten days. More than that, with no serious set-back he may fully recover and live for many years to come."

He was so pleased that tears stood in his one good eye and he wiped them away sheepishly. The girl took his hand and pressed it in both her own.

"You are wonderful—wonderful!" she said.

"Don't, please—don't look in my face," he pleaded.

"I won't," she returned, dropping her eyes; "I will think only of the clever brain, the skillful hand and the stout heart."

"Not even that," he said. "Think of the girl wife—of Elizabeth. It was she who steadied my hand to-day. Indeed, Miss Stanton, it was Elizabeth's influence that saved him. But for her we would have let him die."

CHAPTER XVI

CLARETTE

So it was toward evening of the fourth day that the launch finally sighted the ship *Arabella*. Delays and difficulties had been encountered in spite of government credentials and *laissez-passer* and Patsy had begun to fear they would not reach the harbor of Dunkirk before dark.

All through the journey the Belgian woman and her children had sat sullenly in the bow, the youngsters kept from mischief by the stern eye of Henderson. In the stern seats, however, the original frigid silence had been thawed by Patsy Doyle's bright chatter. She began by telling the countess and Elizabeth all about herself and Beth and Maud and Uncle John, relating how they had come to embark upon this unusual mission of nursing the wounded of a foreign war, and how they had secured the services of the clever but disfigured surgeon, Dr. Gys. She gave the ladies a clear picture of the hospital ship and told how the girls had made their dash to the firing line during the battle of Nieuport and brought back an ambulance full of wounded — including Andrew Denton.

Patsy did not answer very fully Elizabeth Denton's eager questions concerning the nature of her husband's injuries, but she tried to prepare the poor young wife for the knowledge that the wound would prove fatal. This was a most delicate and difficult thing to do and Patsy blundered and floundered until her very ambiguity aroused alarm.

"Tell me the worst!" begged Elizabeth Denton, her face pale and tensely drawn.

"Why, I cannot do that, you see," replied Patsy, "because the worst hasn't happened yet; nor can I tell you the best, because a wound is such an uncertain thing. It was a shell, you know, that exploded behind him, and Dr. Gys thought it made a rather serious wound. Mr. Denton was unconscious a long time, and when he came to himself we eased his pain, so he would not suffer."

111

"You came to get me because you thought he would die?"

"I came because he asked me to read to him your letters, and I found they comforted him so much that your presence would, I knew, comfort him more."

There was a long silence. Presently the countess asked in her soft, even voice:

"Will he be alive when we get there?"

Patsy thought of the days that had been wasted, because of their detention at Ostend through Colonel Grau's stupidity.

"I hope so, madam," was all she could reply.

Conversation lagged after this episode. Elizabeth was weeping quietly on her mother's shoulder. Patsy felt relief in the knowledge that she had prepared them, as well as she could, for whatever might wait upon their arrival.

The launch made directly for the ship and as she came alongside to the ladder the rail was lined with faces curious to discover if the errand had been successful. Doctor Gys was there to receive them, smiling horribly as he greeted the two women in black. Maud, seeing that they recoiled from the doctor's appearance, took his place and said cheerfully:

"Mr. Denton is asleep, just now, but by the time you have bathed and had a cup of tea I am quite sure he will be ready to receive you."

"Tell me; how is he? Are you his nurse?" asked the young wife with trembling lips.

"I am his nurse, and I assure you he is doing very well," answered Maud with her pleasant, winning smile. "When he finds you by his side I am sure his recovery will be rapid. No nurse can take the place of a wife, you know."

Patsy looked at her reproachfully, thinking she was misleading the poor young wife, but Maud led the ladies away to a stateroom and it was Dr. Gys who explained the wonderful improvement in the patient.

"Well," remarked Uncle John, "if we'd known he had a chance, we wouldn't have worried so because we were held up. In fact, if we'd known he would get well, we needn't have gone at all."

"Oh, Uncle John!" cried Patsy reprovingly.

"It was your going that saved him," declared the doctor. "I promised to keep him alive, for that little wife of his, and when he took a turn for the worse I had to assume desperate chances—which won out."

Meantime the big Belgian woman and her children had been helped up the ladder by Henderson, who stood respectfully by, awaiting orders for their disposal. The mother had her eye on the shore and was scowling steadily upon it when little Maurie came on deck and strolled toward Mr. Merrick to greet him on his return. Indeed, he had approached to within a dozen feet of the group when the woman at the rail suddenly turned and saw him.

"Aha—mon Henri!" she cried and made a dash toward him with outstretched arms.

"Clarette!"

Maurie stopped short; he grew pallid; he trembled. But he did not await her coming. With a howl that would have shamed a wild Indian he leaped upon the rail and made a dive into the water below.

Even as her engulfing arms closed around the spot where he had stood, there was a splash and splutter that drew everyone to the side to watch the little Belgian swim frantically to the docks.

The woman grabbed a child with either arm and held them up.

"See!" she cried. "There is your father—the coward—the traitor—the deserter of his loving family. He thinks to escape; but we shall capture him yet, and when we do—"

"Hurry, father," screamed the little girl, "or she'll get you."

A slap on the mouth silenced her and set the boy wailing dismally. The boy was accustomed to howl without provocation. He kicked his mother until she let him down. By this time they could discern only Maurie's head bobbing in the distant water. Presently he clambered up the dock and ran dripping toward the city, disappearing among the buildings.

"Madam," said Uncle John, sternly, "you have cost us the best chauffeur we ever had."

She did not understand English, but she shook her fist in Mr. Merrick's face and danced around in an elephantine fashion and jabbered a stream of French.

"What does she say?" he asked Patsy, who was laughing merrily at the absurd scene.

"She demands to be put ashore at once. But shall we do that, and put poor Maurie in peril of being overtaken?"

"Self preservation is the first law of nature, my dear," replied Uncle John. "I'm sorry for Maurie, but he alone is responsible. Henderson," he added, turning to the sailor, "put this woman ashore as soon as possible. We've had enough of her."

CHAPTER XVII

PERPLEXING PROBLEMS

Although the famous battle of Nieuport had come to an end, the fighting in West Flanders was by no means over. All along the line fierce and relentless war waged without interruption and if neither side could claim victory, neither side suffered defeat. Day after day hundreds of combatants fell; hundreds of disabled limped to the rear; hundreds were made prisoners. And always a stream of reinforcements came to take the places of the missing ones. Towns were occupied to-day by the Germans, to-morrow by the Allies; from Nieuport on past Dixmude and beyond Ypres the dykes had been opened and the low country was one vast lake. The only approaches from French territory were half a dozen roads built high above the water line, which rendered them capable of stubborn defence.

Dunkirk was thronged with reserves—English, Belgian and French. The Turcos and East Indians were employed by the British in this section and were as much dreaded by the civilians as the enemy. Uncle John noticed that military discipline was not so strict in Dunkirk as at Ostend; but the Germans had but one people to control while the French town was host to many nations and races.

Strange as it may appear, the war was growing monotonous to those who were able to view it closely, perhaps because nothing important resulted from all the desperate, continuous fighting. The people were pursuing their accustomed vocations while shells burst and bullets whizzed around them. They must manage to live, whatever the outcome of this struggle of nations might be.

Aboard the American hospital ship there was as yet no sense of monotony. The three girls who had conceived and carried out this remarkable philanthropy were as busy as bees during all their waking hours and the spirit of helpful charity so strongly possessed them that all their thoughts were centered on their work. No two cases were exactly alike and it was interesting, to the verge of fascination, to watch the results of various treatments of divers wounds and afflictions.

The girls often congratulated themselves on having secured so efficient a surgeon as Doctor Gys, who gloried in his work, and whose judgment, based on practical experience, was comprehensive and unfailing. The man's horribly contorted features had now become so familiar to the girls that they seldom noticed them— unless a cry of fear from some newly arrived and unnerved patient reminded them that the doctor was exceedingly repulsive to strangers.

No one recognized this grotesque hideousness more than Doctor Gys himself. When one poor Frenchman died under the operating knife, staring with horror into the uncanny face the surgeon bent over him, Beth was almost sure the fright had hastened his end. She said to Gys that evening, when they met on deck, "Wouldn't it be wise for you to wear a mask in the operating room?"

He considered the suggestion a moment, a deep flush spreading over his face; then he nodded gravely.

"It may be an excellent idea," he agreed. "Once, a couple of years ago, I proposed wearing a mask wherever I went, but my friends assured me the effect would be so marked that it would attract to me an embarrassing amount of attention. I have trained myself to bear the repulsion involuntarily exhibited by all I meet and have taught myself to take a philosophic, if somewhat cynical, view of my facial blemishes; yet in this work I can see how a mask might be merciful to my patients. I will experiment a bit along this line, if you will help me, and we'll see what we can accomplish."

"You must not think," she said quietly, for she detected a little bitterness in his tone, "that you are in any way repulsive to those who know you well. We all admire you as a man and are grieved at the misfortunes that marred your features. After all, Doctor, people of intelligence seldom judge one by appearances."

"However they may judge me," said he, "I'm a failure. You say you admire me as a man, but you don't. It's just a bit of diplomatic flattery. I'm a good doctor and surgeon, I'll admit, but my face is no more repellent than my cowardly nature. Miss Beth, I hate myself for my cowardice far more than I detest my ghastly countenance. Yet I am powerless to remedy either defect."

"I believe that what you term your cowardice is merely a physical weakness," declared the girl. "It must have been caused by the suffering you endured at the time of your various injuries. I have noticed that suffering frequently unnerves one, and that a person who has once been badly hurt lives in nervous terror of being hurt again."

"You are very kind to try to excuse my fault," said he, "but the truth is I have always been a coward—from boyhood up."

"Yet you embarked on all those dangerous expeditions."

"Yes, just to have fun with myself; to sneer at the coward flesh, so to speak. I used to long for dangers, and when they came upon me I would jeer at and revile the quaking I could not repress. I pushed my shrinking body into peril and exulted in the punishment it received."

Beth looked at him wonderingly.

"You are a strange man, indeed," said she. "Really, I cannot understand your mental attitude at all."

He chuckled and rubbed his hands together gleefully.

"I can," he returned, "for I know what causes it." And then he went away and left her, still seeming highly amused at her bewilderment.

In the operating room the next day Gys appeared with a rubber mask drawn across his features. The girls decided that it certainly improved his appearance, odd as the masked face might appear to strangers. It hid the dreadful nose and the scars and to an extent evened the size of the eyes, for the holes through which he peered were made alike. Gys was himself pleased with the device, for after that he wore the mask almost constantly, only laying it aside during the evenings when he sat on deck.

It was three days after the arrival of Mrs. Denton and her mother— whose advent had accomplished much toward promoting the young Belgian's convalescence—when little Maurie suddenly reappeared on the deck of the *Arabella*.

"Oh," said Patsy, finding him there when she came up from breakfast, "where is Clarette?"

He shook his head sadly.

"We do not live together, just now," said he. "Clarette is by nature temperamental, you know; she is highly sensitive, and I, alas! do not always please her."

"Did she find you in Dunkirk?" asked the girl.

"Almost, mamselle, but not quite. It was this way: I knew if I permitted her to follow me she would finally succeed in her quest, for she and the dear children have six eyes among them, while I have but two; so I reposed within an ash-barrel until they had passed on, and then I followed them, keeping well out of their sight. In that way I managed to escape. But it proved a hard task, for my Clarette is very persistent, as you may have noticed. So I decided I would be more safe upon the ship than upon the shore. She is not likely to seek me here, and in any event she floats better than she swims."

Patsy regarded the little man curiously.

"Did you not tell us, when first we met you, that you were heart-broken over the separation from your wife and children?" she inquired in severe tones.

"Yes, of course, mamselle; it was a good way to arouse your sympathy," he admitted with an air of pride. "I needed sympathy at that time, and my only fear was that you would find Clarette, as you threatened to do. Well," with a deep sigh, "you did find her. It was an unfriendly act, mamselle."

"They told us in Ostend that the husband of Clarette is a condemned spy, one who served both sides and proved false to each. The husband of Clarette is doomed to suffer death at the hands of the Germans or the Belgians, if either is able to discover him."

Maurie removed his cap and scratched the hair over his left ear reflectively.

"Ah, yes, the blacksmith!" said he. "I suspected that blacksmith fellow was not reliable."

"How many husbands has Clarette?"

"With the blacksmith, there are two of us," answered Maurie, brightly. "Doubtless there would be more if anything happened to me, for Clarette is very fascinating. When she divorced the blacksmith he was disconsolate, and threatened vengeance; so her life is quite occupied in avoiding her first husband and keeping track of her second, who is too kind-hearted to threaten her as the blacksmith did. I really admire Clarette—at a distance. She is positively charming when her mind is free from worry—and the children are asleep."

"Then you think," said Ajo, who was standing by and listening to Maurie's labored explanations, "that it is the blacksmith who is condemned as a spy, and not yourself?"

"I am quite sure of it. Am I not here, driving your ambulance and going boldly among the officers? If it is Jakob Maurie they wish, he is at hand to be arrested."

"But you are not Jakob Maurie."

The Belgian gave a start, but instantly recovering he answered with a smile:

"Then I must have mistaken my identity, monsieur. Perhaps you will tell me who I am?"

"Your wife called you 'Henri,'" said Patsy.

"Ah, yes; a pet name. I believe the blacksmith is named Henri, and poor Clarette is so accustomed to it that she calls me Henri when she wishes to be affectionate."

Patsy realized the folly of arguing with him.

"Maurie," said she, "or whatever your name may be, you have been faithful in your duty to us and we have no cause for complaint. But I believe you do not speak the truth, and that you are shifty and artful. I fear you will come to a bad end."

"Sometimes, mamselle," he replied, "I fear so myself. But, *peste*! why should we care? If it is the end, what matter whether it is good or bad?"

Watching their faces closely, he saw frank disapproval of his sentiments written thereon. It disturbed him somewhat that they did not choose to continue the conversation, so he said meekly:

"With your kind permission, I will now go below for a cup of coffee," and left them with a bow and a flourish of his cap. When he had gone Patsy said to Ajo:

"I don't believe there is any such person as the blacksmith."

"Nor I," was the boy's reply. "Both those children are living images of Maurie, who claims the blacksmith was their father. He's a crafty little fellow, that chauffeur of ours, and we must look out for him."

"If he is really a spy," continued the girl, after a brief period of thought, "I am amazed that he dared join our party and go directly to the front, where he is at any time likely to be recognized."

"Yes, that is certainly puzzling," returned Ajo. "And he's a brave little man, too, fearless of danger and reckless in exposing himself to shot and shell. Indeed, our Maurie is something of a mystery and the only thing I fully understand is his objection to Clarette's society."

At "le revue matin," as the girls called the first inspection of the morning, eight of their patients were found sufficiently recovered to be discharged. Some of these returned to their regiments and others were sent to their homes to await complete recovery. The hospital ship could accommodate ten more patients, so it was decided to make a trip to Dixmude, where an artillery engagement was raging, with the larger ambulance.

"I think I shall go to-day," announced Gys, who was wearing his mask. "Dr. Kelsey can look after the patients and it will do me good to get off the ship."

Uncle John looked at the doctor seriously.

"There is hard fighting, they say, in the Dixmude district. The Germans carried the British trenches yesterday, and to-day the Allies will try to retake them."

"I don't mind," returned the doctor, but he shuddered, nevertheless.

"Why don't you avoid the—the danger line?" suggested Mr. Merrick.

"A man can't run away from himself, sir; and perhaps you can understand the fascination I find in taunting the craven spirit within me."

"No, I can't understand it. But suit yourself."

"I shall drive," announced Maurie.

"You may be recognized," said Patsy warningly.

"Clarette will not be at the front, and on the way I shall be driving. Have you noticed how people scatter at the sound of our gong?"

"The authorities are watching for spies," asserted Ajo.

Maurie's face became solemn.

"Yes; of course. But—the blacksmith is not here, and," he added with assurance, "the badge of the Red Cross protects us from false accusations."

When they had gone Uncle John said thoughtfully to the girls:

"That remark about the Red Cross impressed me. If that fellow Maurie is really in danger of being arrested and shot, he has cleverly placed himself in the safest service in the world. He knows that none of our party is liable to be suspected of evil."

CHAPTER XVIII

A QUESTION OF LOYALTY

During the morning they were visited by a French official who came aboard in a government boat and asked to see Mr. Merrick.

The ship had been inspected several times by the commander of the port and the civil authorities, and its fame as a model hospital had spread over all Flanders. Some attempt had been made to place with the Americans the most important of the wounded—officers of high rank or those of social prominence and wealth—but Mr. Merrick and his aids were determined to show no partiality. They received the lowly and humble as well as the high and mighty and the only requisite for admission was an injury that demanded the care of good nurses and the skill of competent surgeons.

Uncle John knew the French general and greeted him warmly, for he appreciated his generous co-operation. But Beth had to be called in to interpret because her uncle knew so little of the native language.

First they paid a visit to the hospital section, where the patients were inspected. Then the register and records were carefully gone over and notes taken by the general's secretary. Finally they returned to the after-deck to review the convalescents who were lounging there in their cushioned deck-chairs.

"Where is the German, Lieutenant Elbl?" inquired the general, looking around with sudden suspicion.

"In the captain's room," replied Beth. "Would you like to see him?"

"If you please."

The group moved forward to the room occupied by Captain Carg. The door and windows stood open and reclining upon a couch inside was the maimed German, with Carg sitting beside him. Both were solemnly smoking their pipes.

The captain rose as the general entered, while Elbl gave his visitor a military salute.

"So you are better?" asked the Frenchman.

Beth repeated this in English to Carg, who repeated it in German to Elbl. Yes, the wounded man was doing very well.

"Will you keep him here much longer?" was the next question, directed to Mr. Merrick.

"I think so," was the reply. "He is still quite weak, although the wound is healing nicely. Being a military prisoner, there is no other place open to him where the man can be as comfortable as here."

"You will be responsible for his person? You will guarantee that he will not escape?"

Mr. Merrick hesitated.

"Must we promise that?" he inquired.

"Otherwise I shall be obliged to remove him to a government hospital."

"I don't like that. Not that your hospitals are not good enough for a prisoner, but Elbl happens to be a cousin of our captain, which puts a different face on the matter. What do you say, Captain Carg? Shall we guarantee that your cousin will not try to escape?"

"Why should he, sir? He can never rejoin the army, that's certain," replied Carg.

"True," said the general, when this was conveyed to him by Beth. "Nevertheless, he is a prisoner of war, and must not be allowed to escape to his own people."

Beth answered the Frenchman herself, looking him straight in the face.

"That strikes me as unfair, sir," said she. "The German must henceforth be a noncombatant. He has been unable, since he was wounded and brought here, to learn any of your military secrets and at the best he will lie a helpless invalid for weeks to come. Therefore, instead of making him a prisoner, it would be more humane to permit him to return to his home and family in Germany."

The general smiled indulgently.

"It might be more humane, mademoiselle, but unfortunately it is against the military code. Did I understand that your captain will guarantee the German's safety?"

"Of course," said Carg. "If he escapes, I will surrender myself in his place."

"Ah; but we moderns cannot accept Pythias if Damon runs away," laughed the general. "But, there; it will be simpler to send a parole for him to sign, when he may be left in your charge until he is sufficiently recovered to bear the confinement of a prison. Is that satisfactory?"

"Certainly, sir," replied the captain.

Elbl had remained silent during this conversation, appearing not to understand the French and English spoken. Indeed, since his arrival he had only spoken the German language, and that mostly in his intercourse with Carg. But after the French officer had gone away Beth began to reflect upon this reticence.

"Isn't it queer," she remarked to Uncle John, "that an educated German—one who has been through college, as Captain Carg says Elbl has—should be unable to understand either French or English? I have always been told the German colleges are very thorough and you know that while at Ostend we found nearly all the German officers spoke good English."

"It is rather strange, come to think of it," answered Uncle John. "I believe the study of languages is a part of the German military education. But I regret that the French are determined to keep the poor fellow a prisoner. Such a precaution is absurd, to my mind."

"I think I can understand the French position," said the girl, reflectively. "These Germans are very obstinate, and much as I admire Lieutenant Elbl I feel sure that were he able he would fight the French again to-morrow. After his recovery he might even get one of those mechanical feet and be back on the firing line."

"He's a Uhlan."

"Then he could ride a horse. I believe, Uncle, the French are justified in retaining him as a prisoner until the war is over."

Meantime, in the captain's room the two men were quietly conversing.

"He wants you to sign a parole," said Carg.

"Not I."

"You may as well. I'm responsible for your safety."

"I deny anyone's right to be responsible for me. If you have made a promise to that effect, withdraw it," said the German.

"If I do, they'll put you in prison."

"Not at present. I am still an invalid. In reality. I am weak and suffering. Yet I am already planning my escape, and that is why I insist that you withdraw any promise you have made. Otherwise—"

"Otherwise?"

"Instead of escaping by water, as I had intended, to Ostend, I must go to the prison and escape from there. It will be more difficult. The water route is best."

"Of course," agreed the captain, smiling calmly.

"One of your launches would carry me to Ostend and return here between dark and daylight."

"Easily enough," said Carg. It was five minutes before he resumed his speech. Then he said with quiet deliberation: "Cousin, I am an American, and Americans are neutral in this war."

"You are Sangoan."

"My ship is chartered by Americans, which obliges the captain of the ship to be loyal to its masters. I will do nothing to conflict with the interests of the Americans, not even to favor my cousin."

"Quite right," said Elbl.

"If you have any plan of escape in mind, do not tell me of it," continued the captain. "I shall order the launches guarded carefully. I shall do all in my power to prevent your getting away from this ship."

"Thank you," said the German. "You have my respect, cousin. Pass the tobacco."

CHAPTER XIX

THE CAPTURE

There was considerable excitement when the ambulance returned. Part of the roof had been torn away, the doors were gone, the interior wrecked and not a pane of glass remained in the sides; yet Ajo drove it to the dock, the motor working as smoothly as ever, and half a dozen wounded were helped out and put into the launch to be taken aboard the hospital ship.

When all were on deck, young Jones briefly explained what had happened. A shell had struck the ambulance, which had been left in the rear, but without injuring the motor in any way. Fortunately no one was near at the time. When they returned they cleared away the rubbish to make room for a few wounded men and then started back to the city.

Doctor Gys, hatless and coatless, his hair awry and the mask making him look more hideous than ever, returned with the party and came creeping up the ship's ladder in so nervous a condition that his trembling knees fairly knocked together.

The group around Ajo watched him silently.

"What do you think that fool did?" asked the boy, as Gys slunk away to his room.

"Tell us," pleaded Patsy, who was one of the curious group surrounding him.

"We had gone near to where a machine gun was planted, to pick up a fallen soldier, when without warning the Germans charged the gun. Maurie and I made a run for life, but Gys stood stock still, facing the enemy. A man at the gun reeled and fell, just then, and with a hail of bullets flying around him the doctor coolly walked up and bent over him. The sight so amazed the Germans that they actually stopped fighting and waited for him. Perhaps it was the Red Cross on the doctor's arm that influenced them, but imagine a body of soldiers in the heat of a charge suddenly stopping because of one man!"

"Well, what happened?" asked Mr. Merrick.

"I couldn't see very well, for a battery that supported the charge was shelling the retreating Allies and just then our ambulance was hit. But Maurie says he watched the scene and that when Gys attempted to lift the wounded man up he suddenly turned weak as water. The Germans had captured the gun, by this time, and their officer himself hoisted the injured man upon the doctor's shoulders and attended him to our ambulance. When I saw the fight was over I hastened to help Gys, who staggered so weakly that he would have dropped his man a dozen times on the way had not the Germans held him up. They were laughing, as if the whole thing was a joke, when crack! came a volley of bullets and with a great shout back rushed the French and Belgians in a counter-charge. I admit I ducked, crawling under the ambulance, and the Germans were so surprised that they beat a quick retreat.

"And now it was that Gys made a fool of himself. He tore off his cap and coat, which bore the Red Cross emblem, and leaped right between the two lines. Here were the Germans, firing as they retreated, and the Allies firing as they charged, and right in the center of the fray stood Gys. The man ought to have been shot to pieces, but nothing touched him until a Frenchman knocked him over because he was in the way of the rush. It was the most reckless, suicidal act I ever heard of!"

Uncle John looked worried. He had never told any of them of Dr. Gys' strange remark during their first interview, but he had not forgotten it. "I'll be happier when I can shake off this horrible envelope of disfigurement," the doctor had declared, and in view of this the report of that day's adventure gave the kind-hearted gentleman a severe shock.

He walked the deck thoughtfully while the girls hurried below to look after the new patients who had been brought, not too comfortably, in the damaged ambulance. "It was a bad fight," Ajo had reported, "and the wounded were thick, but we could only bring a few of them. Before we left the field, however, an English ambulance and two French ones arrived, and that gave us an opportunity to get away. Indeed, I was so unnerved by the dangers we had miraculously escaped that I was glad to be out of it."

Uncle John tried hard to understand Doctor Gys, but the man's strange, abnormal nature was incomprehensible. When, half an hour later, Mr. Merrick went below, he found the doctor in the operating room, cool and steady of nerve and dressing wounds in his best professional manner.

Upon examination the next morning the large ambulance was found to be so badly damaged that it had to be taken to a repair shop in the city to undergo reconstruction. It would take several weeks to put it in shape, declared the French mechanics, so the Americans would be forced to get along with the smaller vehicle. Jones and Dr. Kelsey made regular trips with this, but the fighting had suddenly lulled and for several days no new patients were brought to the ship, although many were given first aid in the trenches for slight wounds.

So the colony aboard the *Arabella* grew gradually less, until on the twenty-sixth of November the girls found they had but two patients to care for—Elbl and Andrew Denton. Neither required much nursing, and Denton's young wife insisted on taking full charge of him. But while the hospital ship was not in demand at this time there were casualties day by day in the trenches, where the armies faced each other doggedly and watchfully and shots were frequently interchanged when a soldier carelessly exposed his person to the enemy. So the girls took turns going with the ambulance, and Uncle John made no protest because so little danger attended these journeys.

Each day, while one of the American girls rode to the front, the other two would visit the city hospitals and render whatever assistance they could to the regular nurses. Gys sometimes accompanied them and sometimes went to the front with the ambulance; but he never caused his friends anxiety on these trips, because he could not endanger his life, owing to the cessation of fighting.

The only incident that enlivened this period of stagnation was the capture of Maurie. No; the authorities didn't get him, but Clarette did. Ajo and Patsy had gone into the city one afternoon and on their return to the docks, where their launch was moored, they found a street urchin awaiting them with a soiled scrap of paper clenched fast in his fist. He surrendered it for a coin and Patsy found the following words scrawled in English:

"She has me fast. Help! Be quick. I cannot save myself so you must save me. It is your Maurie who is in distress."

They laughed a little at first and then began to realize that the loss of their chauffeur would prove a hardship when fighting was resumed. Maurie might not be a good husband, and he might be afraid of a woman, but was valuable when bullets were flying. Patsy asked the boy:

"Can you lead us to the man who gave you this paper?"

"Oui, mamselle."

"Then hurry, and you shall have five centimes more."

The injunction was unnecessary, for the urchin made them hasten to keep up with him. He made many turns and twists through narrow alleys and back streets until finally he brought them to a row of cheap, plastered huts built against the old city wall. There was no mistaking the place, for in the doorway of one of the poorest dwellings stood Clarette, her ample figure fairly filling the opening, her hands planted firmly on her broad hips.

"Good evening," said Patsy pleasantly. "Is Maurie within?"

"Henri is within," answered Clarette with a fierce scowl, "and he is going to stay within."

"But we have need of his services," said Ajo sternly, "and the man is in our employ and under contract to obey us."

"I also need his services," retorted Clarette, "and I made a contract with him before you did, as my marriage papers will prove."

The little boy and girl had now crowded into the doorway on either side of their mother, clinging to her skirts while they "made faces" at the Americans. Clarette turned to drive the children away and in the act allowed Patsy and Ajo to glance past her into the hut.

There stood little Maurie, sleeves rolled above his elbows, bending over a battered dishpan where he was washing a mess of cracked and broken pottery. He met their gaze with a despairing countenance and a gesture of appeal that scattered a spray of suds from big wet fingers. Next moment Clarette had filled the doorway again.

"You may as well go away," said the woman harshly.

Patsy stood irresolute.

"Have you money to pay the rent and to provide food and clothing?" she presently asked.

"I have found a few francs in Henri's pockets," was the surly reply.

"And when they are gone?"

Clarette gave a shrug.

"When they are gone we shall not starve," she said. "There is plenty of charity for the Belgians these days. One has but to ask, and someone gives."

"Then you will not let us have Maurie?"

"No, mademoiselle." Then she unbent a little and added: "If my husband goes to you, they will be sure to catch him some day, and when they catch him they will shoot him."

"Why?"

"Don't you know?"

"No."

Clarette smiled grimly.

"When Henri escapes me, he always gets himself into trouble. He is not so very bad, but he is careless—and foolish. He tries to help the Germans and the French at the same time, to be accommodating, and so both have conceived a desire to shoot him. Well; when they shoot him he can no longer earn money to support me and his children."

"Are they really his children?" inquired young Jones.

"Who else may claim them, monsieur?"

"I thought they were the children of your first husband, the blacksmith."

Clarette glared at him, with lowering brow.

"Blacksmith? Pah! I have no husband but Henri, and heaven forsook me when I married him."

"Come, Patsy," said Ajo to his companion, "our errand here is hopeless. And—perhaps Clarette is right."

They made their way back to the launch in silence. Patsy was quite disappointed in Maurie. He had so many admirable qualities that it was a shame he could be so untruthful and unreliable.

As time passed on the monotony that followed their first exciting experiences grew upon them and became oppressive. December weather in Flanders brought cutting winds from off the North Sea and often there were flurries of snow in the air. They had steam heat inside the ship but the deck was no longer a practical lounging place.

Toward the last of the month Lieutenant Elbl was so fully recovered that he was able to hobble about on crutches. The friendship between the two cousins continued and Elbl was often found in the captain's room. No more had been said about a parole, but the French officials were evidently keeping an eye on the German, for one morning an order came to Mr. Merrick to deliver Elbl to the warden of the military prison at Dunkirk on or before ten o'clock the following day.

While the German received this notification with his accustomed stolid air of indifference, his American friends were all grieved at his transfer. They knew the prison would be very uncomfortable for the invalid and feared he was not yet sufficiently recovered to be able to bear the new conditions imposed upon him. There was no thought of protesting the order, however, for they appreciated the fact that the commandant had been especially lenient in leaving the prisoner so long in their care.

The Americans were all sitting together in the cabin that evening after dinner, when to their astonishment little Maurie came aboard in a skiff, bearing an order from the French commandant to Captain Carg, requesting him to appear at once at military headquarters.

Not only was Carg puzzled by this strange summons but none of the others could understand it. The Belgian, when questioned, merely shook his head. He was not the general's confidant, but his fee as messenger would enable him to buy bread for his family and he had been chosen because he knew the way to the hospital ship.

As there was nothing to do but obey, the captain went ashore in one of the launches, which towed the skiff in which Maurie had come.

When he had gone, Lieutenant Elbl, who had been sitting in the cabin, bade the others good night and retired to his room. Most of the others retired early, but Patsy, Uncle John and Doctor Gys decided to sit up and await the return of the captain. It was an exceptionally cool evening and the warmth of the forward cabin was very agreeable.

Midnight had arrived when the captain's launch finally drew up to the side and Carg came hastening into the cabin. His agitated manner was so unusual that the three watchers with one accord sprang to their feet with inquiring looks.

"Where's Elbl?" asked the captain sharply.

"Gone to bed," said Uncle John.

"When?"

"Hours ago. I think he missed your society and was rather broken up over the necessity of leaving us to-morrow."

Without hesitation Carg turned on his heel and hastened aft. They followed him in a wondering group. Reaching the German's stateroom the captain threw open the door and found it vacant.

"Humph!" he exclaimed. "I suspected the truth when I found our launch was gone."

"Which launch?" asked Uncle John, bewildered.

"The one I left with the ship. On my return, just now, I discovered it was not at its moorings. Someone has stolen it."

They stared at him in amazement.

"Wasn't the deck patrolled?" asked Patsy, the first to recover.

"We don't set a watch till ten-thirty. It wasn't considered necessary. But I had no suspicion of the trick Elbl has played on me to-night," he added with a groan. Their voices had aroused others. Ajo came out of his room, enveloped in a heavy bathrobe, and soon after Maud and Beth joined them.

"What's up?" demanded the boy.

"The German has tricked us and made his escape," quietly answered Dr. Gys. "For my part, I'm glad of it."

"It was a conspiracy," growled the captain. "That rascal, Maurie—"

"Oh, was Maurie in it?"

"Of course. He was the decoy; perhaps he arranged the whole thing."

"Didn't the general want you, then?"

Carg was so enraged that he fairly snorted.

"Want me? Of course he didn't want me! That treacherous little Belgian led me into the waiting room and said the general would see me in a minute. Then he walked away and I sat there like a bump on a log and waited. Finally I began to wonder how Maurie, who was always shy of facing the authorities, had happened to be the general's messenger. It looked queer. Officers and civilians were passing back and forth but no one paid any attention to me; so after an hour or so I asked an officer who entered from an inner room, when I could see the general. He said the general was not there evenings but would be in his office to-morrow morning. Then I showed him my order and he glanced at it and said it was forged; wasn't the general's signature and wasn't in proper form, anyhow. When I started to go he wouldn't let me; said the affair was suspicious and needed investigation. So he took me to a room full of officers and they asked me a thousand fool questions. Said they had no record of a Belgian named Maurie and had never heard of him before. I couldn't figure the thing out, and they couldn't; so finally they let me come back to the ship."

"Strange," mused Uncle John; "very strange!"

"I was so stupid," continued Carg, "that I never thought of Elbl being at the bottom of the affair until I got back and found our launch missing. Then I remembered that Elbl was to have been turned over to the prison authorities to-morrow and like a flash I saw through the whole thing."

"I'm blamed if I do," declared Mr. Merrick.

The others likewise shook their heads.

"He got me out of the way, stole the launch, and is half way to Ostend by this time."

"Alone? And wounded—still an invalid?"

"Doubtless Maurie is with him. The rascal can run an automobile; so I suppose he can run a launch."

"What puzzles me," remarked Patsy, "is how Lieutenant Elbl ever got hold of Maurie, and induced him to assist him, without our knowing anything about it."

"I used to notice them talking together a good bit," said Jones.

"But Clarette has kept Maurie a prisoner. She wouldn't let him come back to the ship."

"He was certainly at liberty to-night," answered Beth. "Isn't this escape liable to be rather embarrassing to us, Uncle John?"

"I'm afraid so," was the reply. "We agreed to keep him safely until the authorities demanded we give him up; and now, at the last minute, we've allowed him to get away."

Anxiety was written on every countenance as they considered the serious nature of this affair. Only Gys seemed composed and unworried.

"Is it too late to go in chase of the launch?" asked Ajo, breaking a long pause. "They're headed for Ostend, without a doubt, and there's a chance that they may run into a sand-bank in the dark, or break down, or meet with some other accident to delay them."

"I believe it's worth our while, sir," answered Carg. "The launch we have is the faster, and the trip will show our good faith, if nothing more."

"Then make ready to start at once," said Ajo, "and I'll dress and go along."

Carg hurried away to give orders and the boy ran to his stateroom. Five minutes later they were away, with four sailors to assist in the capture of the fugitives in case they were overtaken.

It was a fruitless journey, however. At daybreak, as they neared Ostend, they met their stolen launch coming back, in charge of a sleepy Belgian who had been hired to return it. The man frankly stated that he had undertaken the task in order to get to Dunkirk, where he had friends, and he had been liberally paid by a German on crutches, who had one foot missing, and a little Belgian whom he had never seen before, but who, from the description given, could be none other than Maurie.

They carried the man back with them to the *Arabella*, where further questioning added nothing to their information. They now had proof, however, that Elbl was safe with his countrymen at Ostend and that Maurie had been his accomplice.

"I would not believe," said Patsy, when she heard the story, "that a Belgian could be so disloyal to his country."

"Every nation has its quota of black sheep," replied Uncle John, "and from what we have learned of Maurie's character he is not at all particular which side he serves."

CHAPTER XX

THE DUNES

The escape of a prisoner of war from the American hospital ship was made the subject of a rigid inquiry by the officials and proved extremely humiliating to all on board the *Arabella*. The commandant showed his irritation by severely reprimanding Mr. Merrick for carelessness, while Captain Carg had to endure a personal examination before a board of inquiry. He was able to prove that he had been at headquarters during the evening of the escape, but that did not wholly satisfy his inquisitors. Finally an order was issued forbidding the Americans to take any more wounded Germans or Austrians aboard their ship, and that seemed to end the unpleasant affair.

However, a certain friction was engendered that was later evidenced on both sides. The American ambulance was no longer favored on its trips to the front, pointed preference being given the English and French Red Cross Emergency Corps. This resulted in few wounded being taken to the *Arabella*, as the Americans confined their work largely to assisting the injured on the field of battle. The girls were not to be daunted in their determined efforts to aid the unfortunate and every day one of them visited the trenches to assist the two doctors in rendering first aid to the wounded.

The work was no longer arduous, for often entire days would pass without a single casualty demanding their attention. The cold weather resulted in much sickness among the soldiers, however, and Gys found during this period of military inactivity that his medicine chest was more in demand than his case of surgical instruments.

A slight diversion was created by Clarette, who came to the ship to demand her husband from the Americans. It seemed almost impossible to convince her that Maurie was not hidden somewhere aboard, but at last they made the woman understand he had escaped with the German to Ostend. They learned from her that Maurie—or Henri, as she insisted he was named—had several times escaped from her house at night, while she was asleep, and returned at daybreak in the morning, and this information led them to suspect he had managed to have several secret conferences with Lieutenant Elbl previous to their flight. Clarette announced her determination to follow her husband to Ostend, and perhaps she did so, as they did not see her again.

It was on Sunday, the twentieth of December, that the Battle of the Dunes began and the flames of war burst out afresh. The dunes lay between the North Sea and the Yser River in West Flanders and consisted of a stretch of sandy hillocks reaching from Coxyde to Nieuport les Bains. The Belgians had entrenched these dunes in an elaborate and clever manner, shoveling the sand into a series of high lateral ridges, with alternate hollows, which reached for miles along the coast. The hollows were from six to eight feet deep, affording protection to the soldiers, who could nevertheless fire upon the enemy by creeping up the sloping embankments until their heads projected sufficiently to allow them to aim, when they could drop back to safety.

In order to connect the hollows one with another, that an advance or retreat might be made under cover, narrow trenches had been cut at intervals diagonally through the raised mounds of sand. Military experts considered this series of novel fortifications to be practically impregnable, for should the enemy defile through one of the cross passages into a hollow where the Allies were gathered, they could be picked off one by one, as they appeared, and be absolutely annihilated.

Realizing this, the Germans had not risked an attack, but after long study of the defences had decided that by means of artillery they might shell the Belgians, who held the dunes, and destroy them as they lay in the hollows. So a heavy battery had been planted along the German lines for this work, while in defence the Belgians confronted them with their own famous dog artillery, consisting of the deadly machine guns. The battle of December twentieth therefore began with an artillery duel, resulting in so many casualties that the Red Cross workers found themselves fully occupied.

Beth went with the ambulance the first day, worked in the hollows of the dunes, and returned to the ship at night completely worn out by the demands upon her services. It was Patsy's turn next, and she took with her the second day one of the French girls as assistant.

When the ambulance reached the edge of the dunes, where it was driven by Ajo, the battle was raging with even more vigor than the previous day. The Germans were dropping shells promiscuously into the various hollows, hoping to locate the hidden Belgian infantry, while the Belgian artillery strove to destroy the German gunners. Both succeeded at times, and both sides were equally persistent.

As it was impossible to take the ambulance into the dunes, it was left in the rear in charge of Jones, while the others threaded their way in and out the devious passages toward the front. They had covered fully a mile in this laborious fashion before they came upon a detachment of Belgian infantry which was lying in wait for a call to action. Beyond this trench the doctors and nurses were forbidden to go, and the officer in command warned the Americans to beware of stray shells.

Under these circumstances they contented themselves by occupying some of the rear hollows, to which the wounded would retreat to secure their services. Dr. Kelsey and Nanette, the French girl, established themselves in one hollow at the right, while Dr. Gys and Patsy took their position in another hollow further to the left. There they opened their cases of lint, plaster and bandages, spreading them out upon the sand, and were soon engaged in administering aid to an occasional victim of the battle.

One man who came to Patsy with a slight wound on his shoulder told her that a shell had exploded in a forward hollow and killed outright fifteen of his comrades. His own escape from death was miraculous and the poor fellow was so unnerved that he cried like a baby.

They directed him to the rear, where he would find the ambulance, and awaited the appearance of more patients. Gys crawled up the mound of sand in front of them and cautiously raised his head above the ridge. Next instant he ducked to escape a rain of bullets that scattered the sand about them like a mist.

"That was foolish," said Patsy reprovingly. "You might have been killed."

"No such luck," he muttered in reply, but the girl could see that he trembled slightly with nervousness. Neither realized at the time the fatal folly of the act, for they were unaware that the Germans were seeking just such a clew to direct them where to drop their shells.

"It's getting rather lonely here, and there are a couple of vacant hollows in front of us," remarked the doctor. "Suppose we move over to one of those, a little nearer the soldiers?"

Patsy approved the proposition, so they gathered up their supplies and moved along the hollow to where a passage had been cut through. They had gone barely a hundred yards when a screech, like a buzz-saw when it strikes a nail, sounded overhead. Looking up they saw a black disk hurtling through the air, to drop almost where they had been standing a moment before. There was a terrific explosion that sent debris to their very feet.

"After this we'll be careful how we expose ourselves," said the doctor gravely. "They have got our range in a hurry. Here comes another; we'd better get away quickly."

They progressed perhaps half a mile, without coming upon any soldiers, when at the brow of a hill slightly higher than the rest, they became aware of unwonted activity. A trench had been dug along the ridge, with great pits here and there to serve as bomb-proof shelters. Every time a head projected above the ridge, a storm of bullets showed that the enemy was well within rifle range. In fact, it was to dislodge the Germans that the present intrenchments were being made; machine guns would be mounted as soon as positions had been prepared.

The German bullets had already taken their toll. In the little valley a poor Belgian pressed his hand against a bad wound in his side, while another was nursing an arm roughly bandaged by his fellows in the trenches. First aid made the two comfortable for the time being at least and the men were directed toward the ambulance. As they left, the man with the wounded arm pointed down the narrow valley to where a deep ravine cut through. "We were driven from there," he said. "The big guns dropped shells on us and killed many; there are many wounded beyond—but you cannot cross the ravine. We lost ten in doing it."

Nevertheless, the doctor and Patsy strode off. Just within the shelter of the ridge they found another Belgian, desperately wounded, and the doctor stopped to ease his pain with the hypodermic needle. Patsy looked across the narrow defile; it was a bare fifty feet, and seemed safe enough. Her Red Cross uniform would protect her, she reasoned, and boldly enough she stepped out into the open. A cry from a wounded soldier ahead hastened her footsteps. Without heeding the warning shout of Doctor Gys she calmly stooped over the man who had called to her.

And then there was a sudden rending, blinding, terrifying crash that sent the world into a thousand shrieking echoes. A huge shell had fallen not fifty feet away, plowing its way through the earthworks above. Its explosion sent timbers, abandoned gun-carriages, everything, flying through the air. And one great piece of wood caught Patsy a glancing blow on the back of her head as she crouched over the wounded Belgian. With a weak cry she toppled over, not unconscious, but unable to raise herself.

Another shell crashed down a hundred yards away, and then one closer that sent the sand spouting high in a blinding cloud. She raised herself slowly and glanced back toward Doctor Gys. He stood, his face ashen with fear, hiding behind the shelter of the other hill. He looked up as she stirred; a cry of relief came to his lips.

"Wait!" he called, bracing up suddenly. "Wait and I will get you."

Bending his head low he sprang across the unprotected space. He stopped with a sudden jerk and then came on.

"You were hit!" cried Patsy as he bent over her.

"It is nothing," he answered brusquely. "Hold tight around my neck." "Now—" another shell scattered sand over them—"we must get away from here."

Breathing thickly, he staggered across the open, dropping her with a great groan behind the protection of the ridge.

"The man you were helping," he gasped. "I must bring him in."

"But you are wounded—" Patsy cried.

He straightened up—his hand clutched his side—there came across his disfigured features a queer twisted smile—he sighed softly and slowly sank in a crumpled heap. A clean little puncture in the breast of his coat told the whole story. Patsy felt herself slipping.... All grew dark.

It was Ajo who found her and carried her back to the ambulance, where Dr. Kelsey and Nanette were presently able to restore her to consciousness. Then they returned to the *Arabella*, grave and silent, and Patsy was put to bed. Before morning Beth and Maud were anxiously nursing her, for she had developed a high fever and was delirious.

The days that succeed were anxious ones, for Patsy's nerves had given away completely. It was many weeks later that the rest of them met on deck.

"It's the first of February," said Uncle John. "Don't you suppose Patsy could start for home pretty soon?"

"Perhaps so," answered Maud. "She is sitting up to-day, and seems brighter and more like herself. Have we decided, then, to return to America?"

"I believe so," was the reply. "We can't keep Ajo's ship forever, you know, and without Doctor Gys we could never make it useful as a hospital ship again."

"That is true," said the girl, thoughtfully. "Now that Andrew Denton, with his wife and the countess, have gone to Charleroi, our ship seems quite lonely."

"You see," said Ajo, taking part in the discussion, "we've never been able to overcome the suspicious coldness of these Frenchmen, caused by Elbl's unfortunate escape. We are not trusted fully, and never will be again, so I'm convinced our career of usefulness here is ended."

"Aside from that," returned Uncle John, "you three girls have endured a long period of hard work and nervous strain, and you need a rest. I'm awfully proud of you all; proud of your noble determination and courage as well as the ability you have demonstrated as nurses. You have unselfishly devoted your lives for three strenuous months to the injured soldiers of a foreign war, and I hope you're satisfied that you've done your full duty."

"Well," returned Maud with a smile, "I wouldn't think of retreating if I felt that our services were really needed, but there are so many women coming here for Red Cross work—English, French, Swiss, Dutch and Italian—that they seem able to cover the field thoroughly."

"True," said Beth, joining the group. "Let's go home, Uncle. The voyage will put our Patsy in fine shape again. When can we start, Ajo?"

"Ask Uncle John."

"Ask Captain Carg."

"If you really mean it," said the captain, "I'll hoist anchor to-morrow morning."